YOUR
TIME
IS
UP

Please note that this book contains themes of eating disorders, self-harm, suicide, drug use, attempted murder and sexual assault.

Published in the UK by Scholastic, 2024
1 London Bridge, London, SE1 9BG
Scholastic Ireland, 89E Lagan Road, Dublin Industrial Estate,
Glasnevin, Dublin, D11 HP5F

Text © Sarah Naughton, 2024

The right of Sarah Naughton to be identified as the author of this work has been
asserted by them under the Copyright, Designs and Patents Act 1988.

ISBN 978 0702 32976 0

A CIP catalogue record for this book
is available from the British Library.

Printed and bound in Great Britain by Clays Ltd, Elcograf S.p.A.

Paper made from wood grown in sustainable forests
and other controlled sources.

MIX
Paper | Supporting
responsible forestry
FSC
www.fsc.org   FSC® C018072

1 3 5 7 9 10 8 6 4 2

www.scholastic.co.uk

YOUR TIME IS UP

SARAH NAUGHTON

■ SCHOLASTIC

For my niece, Sophia Sung,
who has a taste for blood

MISS ZAINA ABBOUR

RECORDED INTERVIEW

Date: 27th June
Time: 12:23
Location: King George's Memorial Hospital
Conducted by officers from the Met Police

ZA: Are they OK?

POLICE: We've had no more updates as yet.

ZA: Well, how long before you know?

POLICE: I'm afraid you'll have to speak to the medical team. Now, for due diligence, we acknowledge that you're not in any fit state to be interviewed, but the nurses said you were insistent—

ZA: Is he dead?

POLICE: For the tape, please clarify who you mean, Miss Abbour?

ZA: It doesn't matter. I need to tell you—

(*ZA cries out in pain and raises hand to head*)

POLICE: I think we'd better leave this until you're feeling better.

ZA: No! You need to know what really happened!

POLICE: There really isn't any rush. What's important is that you—

ZA: No! I have to tell you now! Because otherwise he

will, and he planned this out so well you'll believe him. Sit down. SIT DOWN and listen!

POLICE: It's all right. See, we're sitting down. We're listening. Now, let's just take it easy and start at the beginning, shall we?

ZA: At the beginning? Fine. Let's start there.

The Exam

6:30–8:30

Zaina's face has turned from red to puce, the blood vessels in her eyes are bursting and she hasn't even got the breath to cry for help; she can only make choking, grunting sounds and stare blindly at the white tiles, wondering if she's going to die.

And then the retching finally stops. She flops back against the bathroom wall, feeling likes she's about to pass out. Smacking her head on the toilet bowl and ending up with concussion would not be great for her exam focus, so she concentrates on her breathing and eventually the dizziness passes.

She hauls herself to her feet using the basin. In just

three hours her A-levels will be over. The toughest paper of the most difficult set of exams she will ever take. She can't even imagine how she will feel afterwards, what she'll do with all that time stretching ahead of her like a vast empty ocean.

The Zaina in the bathroom mirror regards her dully, the scraped-back hair emphasizing her sunken cheeks and hollow eyes. She has her father's hair, straight and black – glossy when it's washed but flat and lank if she doesn't pay it enough attention. She has his nose too, and the olive skin that turns yellow when it doesn't get enough sun. Currently, where it isn't flaking, it's breaking out, but on the positive side the disaster of her appearance is an excellent way to ward off any unwanted distractions by way of male attention.

Resting on the plastic shade of the strip light above the mirror is a Gillette razor. It's starting to rust in the damp atmosphere, but no one can bring themselves to throw it away.

She depresses the toilet flush and the little threads of bile that were all she managed to produce slosh away. There was nothing to throw up because she hasn't eaten for nearly twenty-four hours straight, partly because she's had no appetite and partly because that would have meant wasting precious revision time.

There's a tentative knock at the door. "Zai?"

She sighs. Her mum's probably panicking that she's bulimic.

"I'm fine," she croaks.

And she is. She never makes herself sick deliberately, or self-harms, or anything else in the angsty teenage-girl playbook. It's normal to throw up before an exam. She's read about sports stars doing it before matches.

"Thay," the baby says.

"Yes," Mum replies to Zaina's baby sister. "Zai's in there. Tell her to come out and have some breakfast."

"Kickass," says the baby.

The baby's attempts to say "breakfast" usually make Zaina smile, but not today. "I'll be out in a minute."

"OK."

Zaina can hear the unhappy hitch in her mum's voice. She feels a flash of irritation for her mother, who has no idea what it's like to feel real pressure. When she isn't looking after children she's stacking shelves or tidying jumper displays or doing whatever other menial job fits in with school hours. All her twittering about Zaina working too hard is because she doesn't have a clue what you have to do if you actually want to *achieve* something. To make people proud.

When she opens the bathroom door there's a flurry of movement as her mum dashes back to the kitchen to pretend she hasn't really been watching for her daughter to come out.

Stepping over the shoes and toys that litter the cramped hallway, Zaina follows her. The kitchen is a mess, as usual. Dirty crockery and cutlery crowd the small table and the toaster is marooned in drifts of crumbs; her younger brothers are capable of making themselves food but apparently incapable of clearing up after themselves. The sight of the butter-smeared knives and splats of Weetabix do nothing for her appetite.

"Nearly done now," Mum says with faux brightness. Her hair is looking particularly firework-esque this morning, with fuzzy corkscrews shooting off in all directions. With her streaks of grey and worry lines, she looks too old to have a baby. She had Zaina when she was twenty, and then, instead of rectifying that mistake by dumping Zaina in a nursery and going back to college, she and Dad went on to have three more children, the last of whom, Heli, was no more than a barely discernible clump of cells when her dad received his diagnosis. The clump of cells in his own body would, it turned out, grow even faster than Heli did. Three children would have been way more manageable for a single mum.

She feels guilty as Heli comes toddling in and clamps her arms round Zaina's legs. She could never wish her baby sister hadn't been born, but it clearly wasn't sensible to bring a fourth child into a two-bedroom flat, even if you weren't about to become a widow.

Picking her up, Zaina holds Heli listlessly as the baby bats her face with a sticky palm.

"I'll do you some breakfast," Mum says. "What do you fancy?"

"I'm not hungry."

"You have to have something. I could make some porridge."

"I haven't got time for porridge."

"You won't be able to concentrate on an empty stomach. How about toast and Nutella?"

"That's not going to help me concentrate either." Zaina sighs, dumping Heli back on the floor. "I'll just get a massive sugar high followed by a massive low."

Her mum's smile droops.

"Sorry," Zaina says, sinking into a chair. "I'm just a bit stressed. Toast and butter would be great."

Mum comes over and kisses the top of her head. "In the grand scheme of things, they really don't matter. You're going to be fine, whatever happens."

Zaina grunts. Clearly exams *do* matter, otherwise they wouldn't be doing them.

While her mum makes the toast she scrolls through flash cards on her phone, breathing deeply and slowly to quell the panic that's tightening her intercostal muscles and making her stomach ache even more than throwing up did.

$sin(A+B) = sin\ A\ cos\ B + cos\ A\ sin\ B$

She knows the syllabus back to front and upside down. She's done every Paper Three that has ever been published, and if she didn't score full marks (which she usually did), she would go on one of the apps and do question after question until she'd cowed the offending topic into submission.

She's ready. Hopefully readier than Ylsa and Chanelle at any rate.

She ploughs grimly through the toast, flicking the cards as she goes – the Newton–Raphson Method, the trapezium rule, discrete distributions. Mum brings her a glass of orange juice but she pushes it away; she doesn't want to need the toilet in the exam. Her phone alarm warns her she needs to leave in ten minutes. The bus usually only takes thirty to get to college, but she's giving it an hour in case of bad traffic. Abandoning the toast, she gets up from the table.

Out in the hall she checks her pencil case for the umpteenth time – ruler, compasses, pencil, sharpener, protractor and the all-important scientific calculator. Then she closes her eyes and lets what passes for silence in this place wash over her. Above her she can hear Mrs Praed's television, to her left her brothers are blasting each other on the PlayStation, and in the bathroom the shower is dripping. There is one sound missing. Her dad would always insist on having Radio 4 on in the mornings, because it was "educational". Though Zaina wasn't sure what she had ever learned from it, aside from the theme tune to *The Archers*.

Mum comes out. "All set?"

"Yep." She wants to get going now, but she'll have to submit to an embrace or risk hurting her mum's feelings again. Mum walks like an old lady, limping up the corridor as if everything hurts, and puts her arms round her daughter. "I love you, sweetie. We all do. And that's all that matters."

Zaina allows herself to be hugged but she doesn't respond to the ridiculous platitude. If love was all that matters, then Mum wouldn't be sobbing down the phone to the mortgage people.

Her mum pulls away. "I know you'll probably want to be off with your friends straight afterwards…"

Friends? Zaina thinks.

"But let me know how it goes."

"Mm-hm."

"Good luck, baby. Just do your best."

"Ood duck," echoes Heli.

Zaina gives the baby a half-hearted wave, then leaves the flat.

She trudges down the seven flights of stairs to the ground floor and steps out into the morning, shielding her eyes from the glare. It's already hot. In an hour's time, when the sun has fully risen, the exam hall will be unbearable.

When she gets to the bus stop she finds that the display board has stopped working. Opening the app on her phone, she discovers, with consternation, that the 114 isn't due for sixteen minutes. Good job she left herself plenty of time. It's just past seven fifteen and even if it takes the full hour to get to college, she'll have fifteen clear minutes before the exam actually starts. People have even been known to come in late if they've had a problem with transport, but Zaina can't think of anything worse than starting an exam in a fluster like that.

It's impossible to focus on the flash cards as her eyes keep darting up in search of a red shape in the distance. Over the road is the stop for buses coming the other way, from the direction of the college, and also the hospital. The newsagent's behind the bus stop still hasn't replaced the cracked window she fell against after returning from one of the final visits to her dad. It's still covered with cardboard, like the dressing over a wound. Stressed and sleep-deprived and weak from lack of food, she almost passed out as she'd got off the bus, but someone was there to hold her up then. If she faints now, she'll just crash-land on the pavement.

After sixteen minutes and still no bus she starts hyperventilating. She's going to miss the exam, and then the absolute maximum percentage she'll be able to achieve is 66.6 recurring, which will probably be a B or even a

C, which means she won't get into a uni, which means she won't—

The 114 sails round the corner.

Light-headed with relief, she hops from foot to foot until it pulls in, then pushes on before the old lady who was waiting before her. The lower deck is busy so she heads upstairs. There's a fetid smell in the air, and the expressions of the passengers, staring at their phones or fanning themselves with rolled copies of the *Metro*, are uniformly miserable.

A couple of seats near the back are free and she sets off towards them, grasping the poles for balance as the bus jolts forward. One of the free ones is beside a slumbering homeless man. His clothes are filthy, his hair and beard are matted, and she realizes, as she comes level with him, that he is the source of the smell. Her eyes move to the other free seat. The girl sitting beside it smiles and shuffles towards the window to make the space bigger.

Zaina sits down next to the homeless man.

Taking out her phone, she opens the flash cards once more, but it's hard to concentrate with the man's snoring and the sensation of a gaze on the back of her head. She has been studiously ignoring the girl beside the other free seat for over a month, deleting the pleading messages and tearful voice notes, blocking her on socials. What's done is done. Some mistakes you can't come back from.

Competing with the snoring, the penetrating voice of the Tannoy now crackles into life to announce the next stop. Putting her headphones in and finding the playlist she uses as white noise, Zaina starts revising.

If two lines are perpendicular, what must their gradients equal when multiplied together?

The same as a best friendship when one of the parties betrays the other. Zero.

She gets through several hundred cards without a slip before a flash of white outside the window makes her look up. They are passing a large poster advertising veneers: a tanned man grins at her with incisors so white they are almost blue. She has never seen the poster before. And then she realizes that she doesn't even recognize the street they are going down.

She yanks out her earphones in time to hear the end of the fatal announcement that the bus is on diversion. Oh God, why didn't she listen? She could have got off and taken the train. She risks a glance behind her and exhales. Poppy is still on, so they must at least still be going in the right direction. Sensing her gaze, Poppy looks up and tentatively raises her hand. Zaina looks away.

The unfamiliar streets crawl by and then the bus grinds to a halt behind a bin lorry. The traffic is busy now — it's seven forty-five already — and there's no space to overtake, so for the next fifteen minutes they stop and start, stop and start, and the only thing that picks up any speed is Zaina's heart. Staring at her phone, she watches the seconds and minutes flick by, despair descending upon her like the crushing jaws of the bin lorry.

And then, just as she is considering hammering the emergency exit and sprinting the rest of the way, the lorry turns down a side street, the bus accelerates forward, and the college rises into view like a beautiful square concrete phoenix.

Then she realizes it's not really eight fifteen. It's only five minutes past. Since the exams began, she has been setting her watch ten minutes ahead to avoid panics like this. Just as well, because her legs are so wobbly when she disembarks that she has to lean on a lamp post and take some calming breaths before she can even think about walking the last hundred metres to the gates. Descending behind her, Poppy hesitates, as if considering whether to wait for her, then wisely decides against this and walks away.

According to the huge banner fastened to the railings, *Franklyn Roberts Sixth Form College achieves the best A-level results in the borough.* At the end of Year Eleven, her mum thought she should stay on for sixth form rather than move to Franklyn – all her friends were there and it was only a twenty-minute walk from the flat – but she was overridden by her dad. Ninety-seven per cent of Franklyn students get into their first choice of uni, and if you don't pick Oxbridge or a Russell Group, you have to explain yourself to the head.

As she passes through the tall metal gates she glances right, into the car park. Ylsa's white Range Rover is one of the only cars there. It glitters in the sunshine, slewed across two spaces. So, at least one of her academic rivals has arrived in plenty of time and won't begin the exam trembling with adrenaline. With her glossy blonde hair, designer clothes and cosmetically enhanced pout, Zaina didn't consider Ylsa as competition when they all joined, but she's been getting steadily better results over the past two years and is particularly good at exams. Unlike Chanelle, whose nerves often get the better of her and she underperforms. Fortunately. It's a mean thought, but the other two probably feel the same about Zaina.

With the A-level exams limping to their conclusion, the college is eerily quiet, and as Zaina heads for the main building, she disturbs a seagull picking at the litter that has piled up against the corner of the science-block porch. It screeches at her in outrage and flaps off in the direction of the art block at the far end of the campus.

Taking a deep breath, she enters the main building.

Behind the reception desk, Mrs Hatcher, who normally wishes them a beaming good luck on exam days, is on the phone, her expression serious. As Zaina passes, the tail end of the conversation drifts across to her.

"I will certainly let you know if she turns up, yes. Like I say, she was definitely in school yesterday, so I'm sure she's…"

Zaina's stomach lurches with the sudden conviction that she's forgotten her calculator. Her heart doesn't beat for the full four seconds it takes for her to swing her bag off her shoulder and check. The calculator is there. Of course it is.

Pushing through the internal door, Zaina hurries down the corridor to the other end of the building, ignoring

Poppy scurrying past in the other direction. It's only twenty past eight. She still has ten minutes.

Taking the stairs down two at a time, she enters the locker room. She takes out her pencil case, water bottle and the long ruler from her rucksack, then stows the bag in her locker. Ylsa's locker, number 435, is next to hers, and she can see the shadow of her white Mulberry handbag through the grille at the top of the door. Chanelle's is number 76, further down, by the door; the cord from her rucksack dangles from the closed door. Looks like Chanelle made it in good time too.

Feeling eyes on her, Zaina turns round and her gaze locks with a pair of glinting eyes on the other side of the glass doors that lead to the playground.

Mortified, her cheeks flush. Nero Adams has just seen her checking out Ylsa and Chanelle's lockers and he, of all people, will know why, but a tinge of rage slices through her embarrassment. He's smoking. After her dad died, she made him swear to quit, but like everything else that passed between them that vow clearly meant nothing to him.

His lips curve into a smirk as he raises the cigarette to his lips, exposing the smartwatch on his wrist, the one he got for Christmas last year and was so thrilled with. He breathes the smoke out and it curls around his face, like his hair used to before he had the savage crop that makes him look so much older and meaner.

She doesn't want to give him the satisfaction of knowing he has her attention, but she can't seem to drag her gaze away.

He looks good. His skin has a bronze glow, so he must have been out enjoying the sunshine, maybe making up for all the time spent in hospital cafes with their fluorescent lights that gave you an instant migraine and the limp, damp sandwiches that were probably responsible for multiple admissions for gastric disorders. It's the memory of *that* Nero that almost makes her return his smile, but she manages to bite her lip in time.

The spell is broken when a phone starts to ring. It's coming from one of the lockers at the other end of the room.

Turning away, she slams her own locker door and fastens the padlock, then spins on her heel and marches out of the room. Jogging back up the stairs, she gulps down oxygen to try to lower her cortisol levels. She really does not need this kind of stress.

Behind the reception desk, Mrs Hatcher is now frowning down at her phone, but as Zaina approaches she doesn't raise her head to wish Zaina luck or tell her she's a star or utter any of the other warm and fuzzy platitudes the secretary usually comes out with, which for some reason don't annoy Zaina as much as when they come out of her mum's mouth. The door to the right of the reception desk leads to the stairs up to the assembly room, where the exam will be taking place. They need a big room because lots of people take maths. It's the most sensible choice of A-level, as her dad told her when she expressed a tentative interest in art. It opens doors.

She opens the door to the stairwell.

Everyone else is already there and she joins the back of the queue straggling up the stairs, fortunately separated from Poppy by another latecomer. There are twenty or so of them, all displaying varying degrees of nervousness. Some are murmuring and grimacing at each other, others gnaw their fingernails or kick their heels against the wall. A couple shield their eyes from the bars of dusty sunlight falling on them from the tall window like the spotlight of an interrogator.

She is gratified to see that Ylsa, first in the queue, is

pale under her beige make-up. She's twisting hanks of her long blonde hair round her fingers and, judging by the strands clinging to her Chanel jacket, has been doing so compulsively for some time. Zaina heard on the grapevine that Paper Two hadn't gone well for Ylsa, so she will need to ace this one to have any chance of getting the top maths score in the year. Which is, of course, what Chanelle and Zaina will be aiming for too (Chanelle because she's obviously got a fetish for Oxbridge, and Zaina because of the promise). Ylsa's dad runs a very successful construction firm (there are rumours he's a gangster) and Zaina suspects that there might be some parental expectation going on there too: a working-class dad who'll never be accepted into the society his money gives him access to, making sure his daughter will. She was privately schooled all the way from nursery but switched to a state sixth form to have a better chance of getting into a top uni. This is another reason Zaina, whose secondary school was put in special measures twice in the seven years she attended, wants to thrash her.

There's no sign of Chanelle, but in front of Zaina, panting as if they've only just got here too, is Chanelle's partner Saff. The pair have been going out since before Franklyn but had the mother of all rows at Emily Blackwater's party in May. Chanelle might still be a bit wobbly about that, which may affect her performance. Hopefully.

Zaina digs her fingernails into her palm. *Don't be such a bitch.* If she bases her own success on other people's failure, then she's not going to get anywhere.

Mr Peters comes through the red door at the top of the stairs. "Everybody OK? No last-minute panic attacks?"

There are grumbles and groans.

The teacher grins. "You're all prepared; you'll be absolutely fine. And if you balls it up, don't worry – they're hiring at Maccy D's over the road."

Zaina smiles. The young maths teacher is one of her favourites. Firstly because his master's degree is from Harvard and, secondly, because he's fun and supportive. Also, he looks a bit like Harry Styles.

Her smile flicks off when Nero comes through the door and tramps up the stairs to stand behind her in a waft of cigarette stink. He stands deliberately close, probably to try to make her uncomfortable.

"Mr Peters?" she calls. "Smartwatches aren't allowed, right?"

"Correct. Anyone got one on?"

She turns her head towards Nero, drawing Mr Peters' gaze. The teacher comes down, holding out his hand, the fingers twitching. "Sorry, Adams. No looking at porn in an exam."

Any other kid would have got a stern warning, but all the teachers like Nero.

"Sorry, Sir, totally forgot." He hands the watch over without even glancing at Zaina, and she wonders for a moment if she got it wrong. Maybe the smirk in the locker rooms was just a smile. Maybe he wasn't standing too close, maybe she's just being oversensitive.

Whatever. It doesn't matter either way. This is probably the last time she will ever see him. And the tiny twinge this acknowledgement produces in her chest is like the lingering tenderness of a bruise, or the scratchy cough that hangs around after a chest infection. A reminder that you really don't want to pick up that pathogen again.

The door at the bottom opens again and she glances round, expecting to see Chanelle looking pale and harried, but it's Mrs Hatcher. She waddles up the stairs to Mr Peters. "Miss Zita's running late," she pants. "Lost her pass apparently, and she needs it for the car park."

The students glance at one another and there are a

couple of surreptitious fist pumps. Miss Zita is a witch. Last year she accused a boy of looking at another student's work, so his paper was cancelled and he didn't get the grades he needed for uni.

"Can you kick things off on your own, Jon? I could help at a push, but I really need to man the door."

"No, that's fine."

"You won't be able to escort anyone to the toilet before she arrives."

"No cheaters here, Gloria," Mr Peters says loudly. "Right, kiddos?" He cranes his neck at the class, who murmur that they are perfectly trustworthy.

"OK, well, Miss Iggle is in her office in an emergency." She turns and waddles back down the stairs.

Mr Peters glances at his watch, then places a hand on his chest and closes his eyes. "Once more unto the breach, dear friends, once more, or close the wall up with our English dead." Then he opens the red door.

They begin to file through.

A bubble of hysterical laughter swells in Zaina's chest. This is it. It's happening.

The assembly room is large and bright, thanks to the line of windows running along the right-hand side, looking out over the science block. Because of these, on a very hot day the room is stifling and the girls have all learned that it's better to wear trousers than risk spending the exam sitting in a puddle of sweat. All except Ylsa, who favours miniskirts that skim her peachy buttocks.

They file in through the door at the side of the room and each student heads straight for their desk. They've done this twice before and know exactly where they should be sitting. They're used to the idiosyncrasies of the chair and desk, the way each creaks or wobbles, and the students either side of them.

Because of her surname, Zaina is usually at the very back of the room, directly opposite the door and beside the last bank of windows. Picking her way between the other desks she sees her candidate card tacked neatly to the corner of her usual spot.

There's another student in this year group, one she takes chemistry with, whose surname is Able, and in those exams she and Nero are not beside one another, but Enrique Able doesn't do maths, and as she sits down, Nero slides into his own seat beside her, close enough that if they were to stretch out an arm their fingers would touch. She slides the band out of her hair and lets the dark curtain fall down between them. She has no desire to have him in her line of sight while she's working, though, as Mr Peters arranges the spare pens and paper on the invigilator's desk, she snatches a sidelong glance at him. He is frowning down at his paper.

So, the boy who never worries about anything, who thinks the world is one big game for him to have fun playing, is worried about this exam. She tries to feel a sense of schadenfreude but muscle memory gives her another twinge. He really wants to go to Lancaster, and their offer has stipulated an A for maths. She ought to be pleased at the prospect of him screwing up and having to make do with Middlesex. Crushing the treacherous flicker of compassion, she unpacks her pencil case and lines her stationery neatly in the right-hand corner of the desk next to her water bottle.

Between Zaina and the front of the room is a sea of heads: pale, dark, shaved, rainbow-coloured. Pressed against the uncomfortable plastic chairs are bony backs and fleshy backs, many shirts already damp with sweat. Three rows ahead, in the desk to the right of Poppy's, Ylsa is still plucking at her hair, but a desk near the front on the left remains empty.

Where is Chanelle? A last-minute toilet break? If so, she's cutting it fine.

Her eyes dart to the door, willing it to open, and for Chanelle to come tumbling in. They will exchange sour smiles and Chanelle will hurry to her desk and fumble with her pencil case, knowing that Ylsa and Zaina are praying for her to drop everything and have to go crawling about on the floor. But that's the way it should be.

The door doesn't open.

There's a soft squeaking from the front of the room. Mr Peters is writing the times of the exam on the whiteboard behind the invigilator's desk. On the wall above the board is an old-fashioned black flip clock. The bold white display reads 8:26. A couple of the students are dyslexic and will get extra time, but for the rest of them the exam will end in exactly one hundred and twenty-four minutes, or (quick maths) seven thousand, four hundred and forty seconds.

Plenty. She inhales. *A paper never takes that long.* She exhales. She'll probably be done way before the end. Inhale. And might even have time to check her answers. Exhale.

The clock flips to 8:27.

"Can you please fill in your names and candidate numbers?"

There is a quiet scritching as the students answer the easiest question that will be posed to them this morning. Zaina takes the lid off her pen and shakes it to get the ink going. The shaft slots perfectly into the calloused dents in her fingers. As she writes her name and number the last rustles die away and a silence falls. All eyes are on Mr Peters, who has gone very still, his gaze fixed intently on the clock.

8:28.

She runs her forefinger over the gold inscription on the side of the pen: *To Zaina, from Daddy.* She must be the only person in the whole room using a fountain pen, but it has never let her down so far, and she put a new cartridge in last night.

8:29.

The air thrums as twenty teenagers count down the seconds in their heads.

As Mr Peters' lips part, the hairs rise up on Zaina's forearms.

"OK, everyone. You may begin."

The Party

Zaina doubled up, folding at the waist, certain that some unseen assailant had burst from the darkness and punched or even stabbed her. Clutching her abdomen, she staggered out of the bedroom and fell against the banister, gasping for breath. Looking down, she was amazed to see that there was no blood, no evidence at all of the grievous injury. She let her head fall back, staring blindly up at the square of the skylight. The slivered moon was a knife wound in the dark sky.

The floorboards beneath her feet pounded to the beat of the music two floors below and she could hear roaring laughter and squeals of happiness.

On the Snap invite Emily called it the FSH party. *The Fun Stops Here.* Amazing that Zaina was invited at all because the fun usually stopped when someone caught sight of her expression or the droop of her shoulders. But everyone was invited to this one, and everyone came, even the ones who skulked around the college in unsociable huddles, sneering at those, like Emily, who found life such a breeze.

It was hard to dislike the popular kids. They were popular for a reason. Happy enough to be generous with it, to take a chance on the emos and the neeks, the queer crowd and the depressives. Even the bereaved. Emily must have known that these social lepers would end up hiding out in the kitchen or crying in a darkened bedroom but she still gave them a chance. Zaina can't blame her for what's happened. She should have stayed at home.

The moon dissolved as her eyes filled with tears.

Now there was movement from the bedroom behind her: rustling, urgent muttering. The creak of a floorboard.

Pushing herself off the banister she rounded the newel post and stumbled down the stairs, reaching the first-floor landing just as the long shadow fell over her from the floor above.

"Zai! Wait!" The voice was thick with alcohol, the words as clumsy and malformed as Heli's first attempts at language.

Zaina's breath was still coming in sharp gasps, but she found enough of it to yell, "Leave me alone!" before setting off down the next flight of stairs to the ground floor.

It seemed to be a compulsion among her peers to peel the labels from wine and beer bottles, and if she hadn't caught a glimpse of the fairy lights flashing on the curved side of the clear glass wine bottle lying across the last-but-one tread, she might have slipped on it and broken her neck. Spotting it just in time, she managed to vault the last two stairs, landing heavily on the terracotta tiles of the hall, but righting herself straight away and bolting for the front door.

This involved running the gauntlet of the football boys, who predictably enough put their hands on her as much as they could while maintaining plausible deniability. As she pulled away from them they catcalled after her, accusing her of spilling their beer, of being boring and a lightweight.

Bursting out of the house, she staggered into the front garden and sucked in the cold night air, filling her lungs as deeply as she could with the pain in her stomach. On the exhale, a soft wailing sound came from the back of her throat. She had made that sound once before. It was the sound of suppressed grief: grief turned down in volume out of consideration for those around you or because you don't want to attract attention.

Her head was filled with static, but occasionally a channel would tune in and an image would appear. Every detail picked out in the high def of the overhead light in its tasteful wicker shade.

Dizzy, she threw out a hand, clutching blindly for support, and bruised her knuckles on the cold stone of Emily's porch. The only people left to hold her hand now were Mum and Heli. She had to get back to them. To crawl into Heli's cot and let the warmth of her baby sister's body enfold her. The steady beat of Heli's heart was stronger than the pounding bass of the music. She needed her family. What was left of it.

She took a step towards the gate, but her legs were as wobbly as if she had knocked back the whole bottle of Nero's vodka.

Behind her came a thud and a smash, followed by rousing jeer. It looked like her pursuer hadn't been so lucky in avoiding the abandoned wine bottle. But then she was very, very drunk.

To think Zaina had felt bad about that, about leaving her friend to make the shitty decisions she always made when she'd drunk too much. Like piercing her own ear with a needle and a cork or letting Johnny Redman photograph her breasts.

It would be a relief not to have to worry about her any more. Because this was it. The end. The determination restored her strength and she walked purposefully down the path towards the gate. It was still relatively early in the evening. The buses would be running their normal timetable and if she didn't mind changing, she could catch any of the ones that called at the stop over the road.

"Enjoy the party?" The voice came from the shadows by the hedge.

Chanelle Goldstein was standing there smoking. Her mascara had drawn dark lines down her pale face and made it seem like she was trying to camouflage herself against the undergrowth. Her tone of grim amusement didn't stretch to her eyes. In that bloodshot gaze there seemed to be something more vulnerable, almost like an appeal.

But they had far too much history for that.

"Piss off, Chanelle," Zaina said, and stepped out on to the pavement.

She set off in the direction of the illuminated bus stop a hundred or so metres away, concentrating on her breathing and the concrete reality of the pavement beneath her feet – anything other than the images seared into her brain.

Behind her the music became suddenly louder. Someone had come out of the house. The gate clanged and footsteps clattered out on to the pavement.

"Zaina!"

She picked up her pace.

"Zaina, wait! Less talk abow this!"

She picked up her pace.

"I don't unnerstand! I'm not a mind reader, Zai! Come back!"

Poppy was ugly-crying now, but Zaina kept walking. There was a hitch in the footsteps following her, as if Poppy had hurt herself in the tumble down the stairs. In trainers Zaina would easily be able to outpace her, without having to break into an undignified run, but now the tears were coming properly, shattering the lights of the houses and passing cars into bright lozenges of yellow and scarlet.

Poppy's wails were drowned out by the roar of an

engine. The bus that would take Zaina all the way home was rounding the corner at the end of the road. If she ran, she could catch it.

She turned to see whether Poppy could catch up with her in time. Her best friend looked terrible: a beaten-up mess under the harsh glare of the street lamps, top half unbuttoned to reveal her bra, hair tangled and matted, panda eyes, one of her heels bent at a funny angle. After what Poppy had done to her, Zaina should have been glad, but the squalid, pathetic sight was just sickening.

She made it to the bus stop just as the bus was pulling in.

People were laughing and pointing out of the window and, as she boarded and stumbled up to the back seats, she could see why. In her last desperate pursuit of Zaina, Poppy's heel had finally broken and she had fallen over on her backside. As she struggled to get up, her balance awry from alcohol, you could see her knickers and a glimpse of pubic hair. It was humiliating and degrading.

The bus doors closed and the engine roared as it pulled away.

As it passed Emily's house, Zaina saw Poppy struggle to her feet. Removing her remaining high heel she hurled it into a nearby garden, before limping back the way she had come. Chanelle had come out on to the pavement now, and was watching proceedings with an unreadable expression. The bus picked up speed and the two figures began to blur, and then it turned a corner and the scene winked out of sight. Zaina curled herself into a ball and pressed her face against the seat back. The coarse material scratched her face like stubble.

The Exam

8:30–8:45

For a disconcerting moment Zaina cannot process the meaning of the line of words at the top of the exam sheet. The letters and numbers lie there on the page like dead insects that have contorted into shapes in their death throes. All around her she can hear the scratching of pens, the clicking of calculators and the whisk of hands across paper – everyone else has begun. She turns her head and looks out of the window. The seagull from before is standing on the roof of the science block, its white wings spread wide to catch the rays of the sun. Nothing is keeping it there at all. It could just fly away, into the blue. But seagulls probably don't have families and uni offers and the anvil weight of expectation pressing down on their sleek heads.

She sighs and turns back to the paper and after blinking at it a couple of times the meaning of the question finally registers.

Three of the following points lie in the same straight line. Which point does not?
(-2, 14) (-1, 8) (1, -1) (2, -6)

Her shoulders relax. *Easy-peasy.*

Over the next few minutes her pen flies across the page, leaving a confident trail of numbers and symbols as she moves steadily through the questions. She's careful to show all her workings to ensure she gets marks in the unlikely event that the answer is wrong. At the end of question four she risks checking to see how everyone else is doing. Poppy's head is almost touching her desk, her left arm wrapped protectively around her paper – a habit from primary school when the boy next to her used to copy her answers. Ylsa's pen hand is moving slowly and tentatively, as if she's not confident about what she's writing. Chanelle's chair is still empty: even if she comes in now, she'll be at a serious disadvantage. Finally Zaina glances across at Nero … to find him looking right back at her. She jumps and snaps her head back down to the paper.

Question five requires a calculator and she is tapping out the long equation when she becomes aware of movement in her peripheral vision.

Nero's hand is waggling furiously next to his seat.

The sum goes out of her mind. Is he deliberately trying to throw her off? Is this revenge for dobbing him in to Mr Peters about the smartwatch?

Swinging her hair over her left shoulder to block him out, she finishes question five and turns her attention to question six, which is on binomial expansion. There are multiple negatives in the sum, so she needs to think carefully about this one…

But she can't think, because now Nero is making sharp hissing sounds, loud enough to ruin her concentration, but too quiet for the teacher to hear.

Without looking at him, she puts up her hand, and Mr Peters, who is halfway up the aisle beside this one, redirects his steps. He has chosen, considerately, to wear soft-soled shoes, so his footsteps are almost silent. Dropping on to his haunches beside her desk, he whispers, "What's up?" He isn't wearing a tie and she can see down the collar of his pale pink shirt to the fair chest hairs glistening in the sunlight.

"Could you ask Nero to be quiet, Sir? He's distracting me."

The teacher's turquoise eyes darken and he crosses to Nero's desk.

Nero doesn't hiss at her again and she's able to complete the binomial expansion question with relative ease, remembering to include the multiple coefficient *and* the negative indices. She is writing out the final answer in the box when something taps her leg. She jumps and the pen scrawls a jagged line down the paper.

Nero is actually leaning across the aisle, stretching out his ruler to prod her. She bats it away so roughly it clatters to the floor and she glances up in panic. No one seems to have heard. Mr Peters is now walking down the furthest aisle, a line of perspiration darkening the back of his pink shirt. Thank God their desks are at the back of the room, because to any of the other students – Ylsa in particular – that would have looked very much like cheating. Everyone knows she and Nero used to be close, and they might think she was giving him the answers. Is this what he was *trying* to do: get her accused of cheating?

She throws up her arm again. She has to tell Mr Peters what's going on or risk looking like part of it.

As she waits for him to notice, the faintest waft of a familiar scent comes to her: a mixture of deodorant, cigarette smoke and the hair wax Nero favours – the one with the consistency of tar. The fragrance bypasses her brain and travels straight to the ventricles of her heart, setting up a dull ache.

Her raised hand wavers.

Is he really that vindictive?

Lowering her arm, she glances across at him.

He puffs out his cheeks in what looks very much like relief. Then he picks up his paper and jabs his finger at it.

Her head snaps back to the front and she stares at the board. *For fuck's sake.*

Then her brain processes the image that flashed into view.

It was the *front* of the paper, with the exam board logo and barcode at the bottom. Unless Nero has forgotten his own name, what could he possibly have been asking her help with?

Tentatively she slides her eyes back to him.

Look, he mouths. He's pointing to a black speck on the edge of the page, some minor printing error.

She shrugs impatiently. *What?*

He gestures with his two fingers towards his eyes and then across at her desk, which she translates as, *Look at your paper.*

Her heart slams against her ribcage. Is it one they've already done as a practice paper? Is that why she's finding it so easy? If so, someone is bound to let on and then they will *all* have to retake. *Goddamn!*

She looks over at the questions. None of them feel familiar, so she turns back to the front page and tries to work out what the problem is. It's the right paper: *Mathematics Advanced Three.* It has the correct date and centre number. True, there is a printing error halfway down the page, a black splat slightly larger than the one on Nero's, but not enough to obscure any of the writing. This couldn't be grounds to cancel the paper, surely.

She side-eyes him in bewilderment, and then he does something even more bewildering.

Licking his finger, he touches it to the printing error, and slides it down.

She stares.

The speck has become a smear of red.

For a long moment she cannot tear her eyes away from it, and then she hears Mr Peters' unhurried footsteps walking back up the room towards them. He clearly hasn't noticed anything amiss, so she ducks her head and pretends to be tapping into her calculator.

As he passes, she breaks out in a sweat, wondering if he will notice that she's just tapping in random numbers and symbols. But he turns on his heel and starts walking back the way he came, leaving a waft of aftershave in his wake.

She exhales. Her hands are shaking.

Raising the curtain of her hair, she peers across at Nero. His eyes are wide in the sunlight pouring through the windows. On dull days Nero's eyes are hazel, but in the sun they are the deepest gold-flecked green, like a pool in a forest clearing. Not many forests in central London, but once, after their lower-sixth exams, they had taken the train out to Epping, fallen asleep in a patch of dappled shade that disappeared as they slept and got so burned they had to buy bags of frozen peas and press them against each other's shoulders all the way home.

He nods pointedly at her paper. Is he asking her to do the same thing he just did?

The splat of ink is glossier than the rest of the writing, and is actually more brown than black, but aren't black inks made up of all the colours mixed together?

She sighs. The fact is, he probably won't leave her alone until she does what he wants, so she licks her finger and drags it over the misprint.

She stares at the gunshot wound in her paper. A thick line of red now runs down from the black circle. On her fingertip the saliva has dissolved the dried stain into what is unmistakably blood.

But her initial shock soon passes as her rational brain takes over.

The papers were laid out earlier on, either by Mr Peters or Mrs Hatcher, so one of them must have given themselves a paper cut. Hers is always the first paper to be handed out, so it would have been at the top of the pile. If they weren't quite aligned, then the blood would have got on to the edge of Nero's lying directly beneath. Not very hygienic but certainly not worth making a big deal about.

Nero always was too curious by half. Always demanding to know what you were thinking or feeling and why. And Zaina had told him. Everything. The deepest secrets of her heart. Made herself vulnerable, believing that she was safe. That was why it had hurt so much.

She becomes aware of the scratch of pens all around her. Her heart clutches, but when she glances at the clock she sees it's only eight forty. Plenty of time to catch up.

She scowls at Nero, hoping to communicate in no uncertain terms *Leave me alone*, and goes back to the paper. Flipping the bloody page back she turns to where she left off.

Head down. Question seven.

The black ink flows steadily enough but there are one or two more hesitations now, and she can sense the smile creeping across the exam writer's face as they start to drop in some trickier problems with sneaky fiddly bits that are so easy to forget about. So simple to drop a mark here and there, not realizing how many you were accumulating. But Zaina knows, and so far she's pretty sure she hasn't lost any, though she'll be able to tell later when she goes back through the paper in the spare time she always has at the end.

There is a light tap from under her desk.

Has she dropped something?

She peers over the side.

A screwed-up ball of paper is lying on the floor by her foot and Nero is looking pointedly at her.

What the actual fuck?

Mr Peters is currently approaching the invigilator's desk. When he turns and starts coming this way, he will spot the paper and demand to see the contents. If Nero really is trying to shaft her, he will have filled it with answers to make it look as if they are cheating. While it wouldn't make any sense for him to be helping *her*, rather than the other way round, it really isn't worth the risk.

As Mr Peters reaches the desk, she toes the ball back to Nero.

Nero catches it deftly and flicks it back. It makes a louder tap as it strikes the desk leg.

Mr Peters is turning. His handsome profile comes into view, his golden hair glistening in the sunlight.

Lunging down, she snatches up the ball.

As the teacher paces back down the room, she holds it clenched in her fist and scowls at the exam paper, pretending to think while trying to keep her breathing even.

In her peripheral vision she can see Nero bent over his own desk, very still. If he was hoping to get her into

48

trouble, he's failed. But more likely the note just contains another plea for forgiveness.

This is just the sort of thing her dad warned her about. Get involved with boys and it's drama after drama. You get sucked into it, take your eye off the ball academically, and then all your hopes and plans are down the toilet. For the sake of some prick who doesn't actually give two shits about you.

Well, she's had enough. She's reporting him. She doesn't care if he does get disqualified and misses out on his Lancaster grades. Not her problem.

Her hand is halfway up, but then she realizes he might be *hoping* that she'll grass him up so that he can say she asked him for the answers. Surely not, unless in the month they have been estranged he's had a complete personality transplant. Best to check what's actually on the note and make sure.

She waits for Mr Peters to reach the end of the aisle on the other side of Nero, make the turn and set off in the opposite direction, his trainers whispering against the parquet. Then she unfurls her hand. The ball of paper is damp with the sweat from her palm. Checking that no one else is looking, she notices Ylsa's elbow see-sawing as she crosses something out so savagely she knocks one of her pencils to the floor. Hopefully she's having too much trouble to be interested in what anyone else is doing.

Zaina unfurls the paper and flattens it out on her desk.

Toilets in 5

Turning to Nero, she gives an incredulous snort and raises the paper in disbelief. *Are you fucking kidding?*

But Nero isn't looking at her. He's looking towards the front of the room with an expression of alarm.

She follows his gaze. Mr Peters has stopped to pick up a dropped rubber and now he's straightening up and looking directly at her. He's seen the note. He is coming this way.

Her heart stops.

This is it. Nero really has screwed her, though his alarmed expression suggests it might not have been deliberate. No time to think about that now. Mr Peters is coming and he will want to know exactly what it is they were planning to do in the *toilets in 5*, especially since they can't be escorted there because of Miss Zita's absence. Her mind blanks. How the hell can she explain? And even if she tells the truth, he's not going to be sympathetic about them bringing their personal problems into the exam hall. She'll be disqualified. *Bye-bye* top-flight uni. *So long*, well-paid job in finance that had been her dad's dream for her. Gasping for air, she realizes she's heading into a full-blown panic attack.

But then, as Mr Peters comes level with a desk a few rows down, he slips on Ylsa's pencil.

He tries to stay on his feet but he's too unbalanced. The arm he throws out to save himself knocks the desk on the other side of him and the stationery goes flying. He sprawls forward, landing on his hands and knees on the parquet, as pens and pencils clatter around him like hailstones.

There are a few repressed titters as he stays where he has fallen, stunned.

And then the solution to the problem beams into Zaina's head like a shaft of sunlight. Screwing up the scrap of paper into a ball, she stuffs it into her mouth. It's too big to swallow dry, so she snatches up her bottle of water to wash it down. It goes down a little way but then becomes wedged in her throat.

She carries on drinking, but though the water passes down her gullet the ball remains stuck.

As she starts to choke, she considers whether death by

maths exam might actually be a good way to go. At least she'd be remembered.

But she keeps glugging and finally the ball softens enough to shift, passing sluggishly down her oesophagus and allowing the oxygen to follow.

Gasping and on the verge of tears, she looks up, expecting to find the teacher standing over her with his arms folded, or possibly one outstretched and pointing towards the door. But Mr Peters is still crawling about on the floor, picking up the stationery.

She has a second or two more.

Hurriedly Zaina tears out half the final page of the exam paper, the one you're supposed to use if you need extra space for working. After scribbling random numbers on it, she screws it up, and puts it down next to her water bottle.

One minute later a slightly flustered Mr Peters finally arrives at her desk, shirt half untucked, and holds out his hand.

With a look of ingenuous surprise, she hands over the screwed-up page, filled with symbols and crossings-out.

Please don't notice that they bear no resemblance to any of the questions.

"I realized I got all the workings wrong," she whispers desperately. "I tore the page out because I was so angry with myself."

She holds her breath as he scans the scrawled numbers filling the page, then he gives a little snort. "I'm not surprised." Putting the paper back down on the desk, he shakes his head and walks away.

She exhales like a competitive free-diver breaking the surface. *Thank you, God, Jesus, Allah, Yahweh, Buddha, Brahman and all the saints of Heaven, Paradise and Valhalla.*

Without looking at Nero, she pointedly clamps her middle finger to her cheek, then settles back to work.

The sun is fully up now, but fortunately her desk is at the end of the bank of windows, so she is shielded from the full glare. Ylsa is getting it full in the face, and her blonde hair burns like white flame. Seeing the other girl's shoulders rising and falling as she stress-pants gives Zaina a pang of guilt. They are all in this together. It's a shame she, Ylsa and Chanelle couldn't have supported one another more. If they'd had a *may the best girl win* approach rather than *live and let die, preferably painfully*, the past year would have been considerably easier. She wouldn't have walked into every maths lesson with a tightness in her chest, knowing she couldn't get one of Miss Zita's questions wrong or they would gloat. She wouldn't have had to check every peer-marked test to make sure she hadn't been deliberately scored down. But she could hardly blame them for that. She was just as bad herself.

That's something Nero would never do. He is always happy for other people's successes. She used to tease him about it, for being a weirdo; everybody felt envy and resentment. But not him, apparently. She's only seen him bitter and disappointed once.

There she goes again, letting a boy distract her from what's important.

She twists the pen so that the inscription faces her. The font is elegant but the way the laser has cut it into the wood of the shaft has left sharp edges. She runs her thumb over them.

She's got this. *For you, Dad.*

The Party

The phone alarm went off. She'd been revising physics in her bedroom for fifty-five minutes, so it was time for the five-minute break that would help her stay focused for the next fifty-five.

When she got up from the chair her back cricked. So did her knees and her neck. In fact, everything cricked. She felt like an old lady. She *looked* like an old lady she decided, as she gazed at her reflection in the bedroom window, which had become a mirror against the night. More like her father than she was comfortable with, and not the father that dunked her in the sea in Camber Sands or won the egg and spoon race at her brothers' school fair (before triumphantly eating the egg in question whole, to her mother's horror). No, the father with the yellow skin and the patchy hair, who only had the energy to stare listlessly at *Homes Under the Hammer.*

Her eyes shifted focus to the street below. The rush hour was just starting to tail off, but at this time on a Friday night there were plenty of pedestrians on their way to bars and restaurants. A girl who looked a bit like her hurried under a street lamp and the sequins of her dress glittered like stars.

Her mind strayed back to Newtonian mechanics and the problem of how celestial bodies interacted with one another. Her dad had encouraged her to take physics A-level along with maths. A dream combination, apparently, that would open up any number of well-paid careers. After that, it made sense to choose another science, so she picked biology, not that it interested her much, and the transcription and translation topics did her head in.

She forced the work thoughts from her brain. This was her break. If she didn't use it properly, she wouldn't be able to concentrate. The exams started in less than a month. Only someone who didn't give a damn about their future would be out partying on a night like this. Which is why she was not.

The brake lights of the cars red-shifted away from her, the universe forever expanding, every celestial body becoming more distant from every other, until at some point in the future every particle in the universe would exist alone in an infinity of darkness.

No physics! She had to think about something else.

Crossing the small room in two steps she picked up her phone from where it was charging on the carpet, intending to numb her brain with a doom scroll.

There were seventeen messages waiting for her. Five were from Poppy, the others were on the FSH party chat.

She felt strange about Poppy and Nero going to the party without her. As if some primitive, irrational part of her brain had decided that if *she* was suffering, then her best friends should as well. Normally they would have done, especially Poppy.

They'd been inseparable since the first year of secondary school. When Zaina knew she was going to Franklyn for sixth form she'd begged Poppy to come too. She hadn't taken much persuading; neither could imagine being apart from one another, having new experiences that the other wouldn't be sharing. It was such an intimate relationship. They didn't just finish one another's sentences, often they didn't even need to speak to know what the other was feeling. Of course, as they grew older, their personalities started to diverge. Poppy was impulsive, spontaneous, occasionally lacking judgement, while Zaina was serious, studious, overcautious, but even this had felt like two sides of the same coin. Over the years they had been through everything together.

Zaina highlighted Poppy's hair and Poppy painted Zaina's toenails.

Zaina microwaved the heat pack when Poppy's period pains were bad and Poppy plucked the hairs from the mole on Zaina's back.

When Poppy broke her ankle, Zaina pushed her around school in a wheelchair, and when a Year Nine boy bullied Zaina about her faith, Poppy punched him and got suspended.

And then Zaina's dad died.

The way Poppy looked at her afterwards, with frightened, uncomprehending eyes, was the first time Zaina had really understood that they were separate people. Ever since then Zaina had watched Poppy moving away from her, as if she was looking at her through the rear-view mirror of a car travelling into a strange bleak country. A country that Nero, who she'd known for little more than a year, had accompanied her to.

In order to lose the party notifications, she opened the chat and glimpsed the last few messages. Most of them were pictures: wide-angle lens shots of girls applying mascara, extreme close-ups of glossy lips, people kissing and dancing and swigging beer. In one of the shots she could make out Nero laughing with some boys from the football team. Her lips twitched in a smile. Nero was just as comfortable with the popular kids and the jocks as he was with the nerds. She expanded the photograph with her fingertips. He was wearing the T-shirt she had got him, with the picture of two fly agaric mushrooms growing from the same root. When her dad was really ill, Nero would come over and work with her at the hospital, only going home to sleep. Sometimes neither of them would see the sun for days. He said they were like mushrooms growing together in the darkness.

She gazed at the picture wistfully. God, she'd love a beer. And she'd love to remember how to laugh again. But that wasn't important now. She had made a promise.

Exiting the group chat, she read Poppy's messages.

7:50 Gonna leave in 10 mins. U changed your
    mind yet??

8:36 Come! It's fun!

8:36 You don't have to stay late!

9:08 Pleeeeeeeeeeeeeeeeeeeeeeease! I missss
    yooooooooooo

9:11 Cmon. Itll do ugood 2 hav a brake!!!!

The later messages were stacked with emojis. Presumably Poppy was drunk by the time she sent them. Zaina closed the app.

Peer pressure. Another thing her dad had warned her about in those interminable final days.

"They'll tell you 'it's not healthy', that 'cramming doesn't work', that 'if you don't know it now, you never will'. It's what low achievers say to make themselves feel better, and it's all absolute rubbish. They just want you to be like them, and you're not. You're special, Zai; you've got such potential."

Zaina had smiled as he clutched her hand and squeezed it with all the strength left in his own yellowed claw, his skin dry and feverishly hot.

"I knew it from the day you were born. The way

60

you looked at me with those bright, curious eyes. I just knew."

She'd heard this before, many times, in fact, in those last few weeks, always said with a kind of febrile intensity. Her dad's own father had died a couple of years ago, from the very cancer that was now eating him, but Granddad never told his kids what was happening, and the end when it came was so sudden Dad didn't have the chance to tell him all the things he wanted to. *He* wasn't going to make the same mistake. This was his last chance to tell Zaina everything he'd thought he had a lifetime to impart to her. The first thing he'd done, when he found out the prognosis, was to buy all these books with names like *The Book You Wish Your Parents Had Read* and *Saying Goodbye Too Soon*.

She knew that he talked to the boys about *what it meant to be a man*. Whatever that was supposed to be. Weren't all men different, like all women?

She'd tried to listen, to take it all in and commit it to memory, knowing how important it was, but sometimes she wished they could just have a laugh over random TikToks like they used to. A lot of times, in fact.

The last day, they all knew it was going to happen. Most of the time he was asleep and when he was awake he was away with the fairies from the morphine. In the afternoon Mum took Heli and the boys for a walk in the hospital gardens, leaving Zaina alone with him. He woke up and she could tell he was in pain, but when she went to pull the cord for the nurse, he stopped her. That was when it happened.

He grasped her hand and brought it up to his bony chest. "There she is. My clever girl. A chip off the old block, aren't you, eh? I was just like you at your age. I had such potential. But I wasted it."

"No, Daddy," she whimpered. "You didn't. You had us."

"I was a whizz at maths, just like you. They said I should go to university, but I'd fallen in love with your mum. At that age that's the only thing that matters."

He paused to catch his breath. The whites of his eyes were nicotine-stained and threaded with veins. "Then you grow up. You realize that other people, those who didn't have half your brains, are living these wonderful lives."

"Our life was wond—"

"Fabulous holidays, private schools, second homes, and just because they worked harder in those few short years when it really mattered."

He went on to list the people he'd been to school with

who had done better than him. The commodities trader, the construction company boss, the corporate lawyer.

"Their parents understood the way the world worked, what you had to do to get on in life. Mine didn't."

"Granny and Granddad worshipped you, Dad..." She hated contradicting him, but she couldn't bear him to trash her beloved grandparents. They had been fun and loving, building sandcastles with them at Camber, taking them to the panto and to see Father Christmas at Harrods.

"But they never pushed me. And they should have. Then I could have *been* something. I could have given you everything you deserved."

"Daddy, you did."

"I've always pushed you, haven't I? Because I know what you're capable of, and I know you'll make me proud. Won't you, eh? Make your daddy proud?"

She nodded like a bobble-head as he stared at her with his bulbous yellow eyes. And then the others came back and he started breathing funny. The boys and Heli went out with the nurses, but Zaina wouldn't leave Mum, so they'd stayed and listened to that terrible breathing for another hour that felt like a hundred years, and then he died. Without saying anything else to her.

Just that. *Make your daddy proud.*

It just wasn't a last wish, of course. It was a vow more binding than a blood pact. Break that sort of a promise to your dying parent and you not only go to hell, but you live there for the rest of your sorry guilt-blighted life.

But that wouldn't be her, she thought, dropping the phone back on the carpet, because she *would* make him proud. She would fly higher than he could ever dream, to the very top; she would be someone special, someone who *mattered*.

Her eyes filled with tears, though they were no longer from grief but a kind of helpless panic. How would she ever *know* if she was making him proud? When would it ever be enough?

Her phone lit up in her hand.

Her heart shed its outer layers of dust and gas and glowed. Nero.

Get here now or Ill come over there and drag u out

She tapped out a reply. Gotta work

The response was instant. Bullshit. Youve worked so hard your hair is falling out

64

This was true. It was just another thing that kept her dad, who lost all his hair during chemo, front of mind at all times.

Come out now or Im reporting your mum to
social services

Not funny

Not joking. Seriously. U need this

He was right. She did need a break. But it wasn't just work stopping her.

She didn't know what to say to normal people any more. *Do you like my new trainers? Did you see the TikTok about [insert youth culture reference here]? What's the Reading line-up?* It all sounded almost comically pointless and she couldn't quite believe *she* used to say the same things.

Since then a veil had been torn away, and what she had seen on the other side of it she could never unsee. She could no longer pretend that the world was a safe, happy place, and that separated her from everyone else who got to live under the comfort blanket of ignorance. Well, almost everyone.

Nero was typing again. Longer than he would need to write the four words that eventually pinged through.

Please. I miss you.

It was the same thing Poppy said, but for some reason this time it worked.

Ten minutes later she walked into the living room. Her mum was watching some Marvel series with her brothers. Cameron turned round and grimaced. "You look stupid."

"What, just cos I'm not wearing full Captain America cosplay?"

She was in her cut-off shorts and a cropped T-shirt, which would look a lot better if the strip of exposed stomach wasn't at the so-white-it's-blue end of the spectrum.

"You're gonna snog someone." Kieran chortled, then made exaggerated lip-smacking noises, to which Cameron responded by retching.

Her mum was smiling. "You're going to the party?"

Zaina shrugged. "Nero and Poppy want me to."

"Good!" Mum got up and came over, batting her hands, as if to physically thrust her out of the door. "Go!"

She backed out into the hall. "I won't be late."

"*Do* be late!" Mum cried. "Pull an all-nighter!"

"So I can have a pounding headache all day tomorrow and not be able to revise?"

"One day off won't kill you, Zai."

Zaina sighed and thrust her feet into her DMs. "I'll see you later."

"If you miss the last bus, get an Uber back."

She rolled her eyes. They couldn't even afford to replace Heli's broken pushchair. "I won't miss the bus."

The Exam

8:45–9:00

She's in flow, the numbers pouring out of her through the conduit of the pen, as if her blood has turned to ink. She can almost feel her dad smiling down at her. This is what she was meant to do, this is what would have made him happy. She could carry on for ever, immersed in the simple logic of numbers, which always behave exactly as you expect them to.

And then she comes to a problem she's not sure how to solve. There must be a familiar method in here somewhere, but the wording is so obscure that she can't figure out what it is she's being asked to demonstrate. Fingers of dread close round her throat. It's a four-marker. She reads it through for the third time then turns to the formula sheet, her gaze skittering across the complex arrangements of numbers and letters, symbols and brackets. Finally she realizes. It's a simple enough example of the Newton–Raphson Method. She has begun to insert the information provided in the question into the formula when she becomes aware of Mr Peters' approach. He crouches beside Nero's desk and a whispered conversation begins.

"What is it, Nero?"

"Can I go to the toilet?"

"I'd rather you wait. I'm here on my own until Miss Zita gets here."

"I'm desperate. I had a whole can of Monster before I came in. I won't be long, but it's getting so I can't concentrate. I'm not trying to cheat or anything. You can trust me, Sir."

This is probably true. Nero has never been one of the really bad kids – the ones who shoplift from the local stores or fight with the kids from the neighbouring schools – and he's playing to that advantage. His face is completely ingenuous.

Mr Peters sighs. "You've got five minutes. Literally a second longer and I'll have to disqualify you. It's not fair on the other students."

"I'll be back before you know it."

"Go on then."

Zaina keeps her head bent as Nero gets up and his footsteps recede across the floor, but when she hears the squeak of the door hinges, she can't resist glancing over and their eyes meet. She can read him like a book. He might as well have uttered the word out loud. *Coming?*

She looks away, returning to the paper and completing what is definitely the most difficult question yet, pretty certain she's bagged the whole four marks. Before she embarks on the next one, she tugs up the waistband of her trousers to stop it pressing on her bladder, which is filling up after downing the whole bottle of water. Maybe she'll sweat it out before she starts really needing to go. The room has warmed to an uncomfortable level. There's a changing-room smell of antiperspirants working at full capacity and her thighs, encased in black polyester trousers, are starting to sweat. So is the hand crabbed round her pen. Laying it down momentarily, she wipes her hand on her trousers, then wafts it around to dry. There's a dent in her middle finger, a ridge where the pen sits, that never really goes away now. Sometimes, if she's been gripping it hard, she can read the mirror image of the inscription in her own flesh.

From one of the desks towards the front of the hall a sound drifts across to her. One that should please her.

Ylsa Marchant is sniffling, hunched over her desk, her hair spreading out like a puddle of golden tears. Has she stumbled on the Newton–Raphson Method too? In which case Zaina will already be four marks ahead, one step closer to the maths prize. And yet, really and truly, Ylsa has never been a real rival for the top spot. She's slow on the uptake and has to go over a new method several times before she gets it. By the next lesson she's usually up to speed, but probably only because she's gone over and over it at home. That means she's OK on questions she recognizes but often stumped by anything that requires more lateral thought.

Zaina's only real competition is Chanelle, and it looks like Chanelle's going to miss the paper entirely, losing a third of the marks available at a stroke. If it was for a proper reason, like an accident or family emergency, she might be allowed to resit on the contingency day, but her bag was in her locker, so it looks like she made it into school and then had a wobble.

But a wobble for Chanelle could mean more than tears or stress-vomiting. Once, early in lower sixth, Chanelle made the mistake of wearing bell sleeves and when she put

72

her hand up to answer a question, the sleeve slipped down to her elbow. She snatched her hand down but it was too late. They had all seen the scars.

The thought of Chanelle locked in a toilet, somewhere on campus, makes Zaina a little uneasy. Shouldn't someone be looking for her?

Nero's been gone quite a long time now, so maybe he ran into her. She finds herself glancing at the door, hoping that he will hurry back in to alert Mr Peters, that Chanelle will be ushered into the exam room and given extra time to complete the paper. Fortunately the teacher doesn't seem to have noticed how long Nero has been, as he's preoccupied trying to get Tyler James's calculator to work.

The inscription on her pen catches a hangnail on her middle finger, as if her dad is trying to get her attention. *Don't worry about what everyone else is doing. Keep your eyes on the prize.* It's her mum that's always concerned about everyone else: that the students are too overworked, that their mental health will suffer. Her dad, and then Zaina herself, had to explain that this is the way the world works. *If you can't hack it, there'll be a million other driven kids who'll happily take your place.*

Ylsa's sniffles have descended into full-blown sobs.

Others in the exam hall are looking over at her now, including the new girl who had some kind of beef with Ylsa at the party. You'd never have known from their behaviour afterwards – Ylsa was her usual poised self and Tabitha remained watchful and reserved, but Zaina had witnessed it first-hand.

Finally Mr Peters notices. Abandoning Tyler's calculator, he crosses the room to Ylsa's desk and crouches down, talking quietly to her, a reassuring hand on her back.

Ylsa nods rapidly, gets up from the desk, and hurries to the door, colliding with at least two desks on the way.

Nero still hasn't returned from the toilet, so they might bump into each other, which surely can't be allowed.

Zaina shifts in her seat to try to ease the pressure on her own bladder.

Settling into the next question, she starts untangling it knot by knot until there is just a single straight thread from the start to the finish, and is struck again by how obedient and predictable numbers are. You feed in the integers and the answer comes out the same every time. Feed two humans the same diet and one will be fine and one will get bowel cancer. Her dad always thought he'd got sick because of all the sausages, bacon and burgers Granny fed him as a kid, but Mum said everyone ate that stuff when they were young. She only said this once, though, because Dad's mood took such a nosedive. Zaina understood. He needed a reason for what happened to him. For it to just be random would be unbearable.

Life isn't fair, but numbers are.

She's writing the final answer, ninety-nine per cent sure she's got it right, when the pen slips through her damp fingers and clatters to the floor. As she bends to retrieve it, the hints from her bladder become more insistent.

The next question is a six-marker and she'll really need to concentrate. If she goes to the toilet now, she'll be able to focus better and in the long run this is probably a much more sensible idea than trying to hold it in. Glancing at the clock above the invigilator's desk, she sees it's only just coming up to nine. That's fine. She normally does a whole paper in an hour and a half and she's well into this one already.

She puts up her hand, and while she waits for Mr Peters to notice, her eyes skim the room and catch on Saff Jackson's pale blue crop. They too have taken a break from the paper and, though Zaina can only see the back of their head, their gaze seems to be directed towards Chanelle's empty chair. There is something terribly forlorn about the abandoned desk, with its paper still sitting there, like a loyal dog never quite giving up hope of its mistress's return.

Zaina glances at the door again. If Chanelle came now, she'd still have the time to get through a good chunk of the paper.

Say Zaina does manage to get the top mark for maths, the victory will be a hollow one if Chanelle hasn't sat all the exams too. She finds herself wondering if Chanelle has done this deliberately. Knowing she didn't do well in the first two papers, is she throwing a sickie to make sure there will always be a question about Zaina's success? *Ah, but what if Chanelle Goldstein hadn't been ill that day…?*

God, listen to Miss Conspiracy Theory. Nero isn't trying to ruin her chances and nor is Chanelle. Other people have other shit going on. It's not all about her.

Mr Peters arrives at her desk. "What's the matter, Zaina?"

"I'm really sorry, but I need the toilet too."

He gives a huff of exasperation. "Can't you wait? Nero and Ylsa have gone already."

She squirms in her seat. With the prospect of imminent relief, her bladder's demands are becoming strident. "I really don't think I can, Sir. I swear I won't say a word to either of them. I'll just be in and out. You can time me; I won't even need five minutes."

Mr Peters rubs his temple, where tiny droplets of sweat are beading. Perhaps he thinks there's a mass scam afoot that he'll get the blame for.

"Honestly, Sir. You know how much me and Ylsa want to beat each other." She gives a grimacing smile.

Mr Peters glances at the door. "Well, they've both been gone a while now, so they're probably on their way back." He looks at her. "Not a word is to pass between you, OK? Don't even look at each other."

"I promise."

He rolls his eyes and she gets up from the chair and scampers for the door.

It's a short dash up the corridor from the assembly room to the cubicle toilets. These used to be the girls' ones, but now they're supposed to be for everyone. Opposite are the urinal toilets, which are also communal since there is the one cubicle, but there's no way any of the girls would venture into that stinking swamp. She feels sorry for the trans boys, of whom there are three in the school, used to a more civilized experience before their transition, who must now deal with urine-pooled floors and wads of poopy toilet paper stuck to the ceiling.

She doesn't mind bumping into Ylsa – they will happily ignore one another – but she's dreading seeing Nero. To be gone this long, he must be waiting for her.

Keeping her steps light, she tiptoes past the door to the urinal toilets and slips into the cubicle ones, letting the door close silently behind her. It's refreshingly cool in the gloomy bathroom. One of the doors is engaged, so Ylsa must still be here.

Against the wall is a bank of basins under a large mirror. It's where the popular girls stand to do their make-up, so the laminate between the sinks is liberally stained with foundation, mascara and blobs of nail varnish. A cold tap in the middle sink has been stuck on for weeks now, and the rushing noise masks any sounds of distress that might be coming from the occupied cubicle. Zaina wonders whether to knock and ask if Ylsa's OK, but Ylsa would be convinced that any display of sympathy was fake. In her position, Zaina would too. They've treated one another like the enemy for the past two years. Did the toxic atmosphere all get too much for Chanelle? Is that why she didn't show up today?

Turning to lock the cubicle door after stepping inside, she catches sight of her reflection in the mirrors above the basins. Strands of sweat-damp hair are plastered to her temples, her eyes are bloodshot, her skin is shiny and patches of sweat are spreading out from under her arms. A part of her is sorry that Nero has seen her looking like this, but she hasn't got time to dry herself under the drier and she wouldn't want to alert Ylsa to her presence anyway.

Sliding the bolt silently across she sits down, adjusting her position so that the pee hits the side rather than splashing loudly into the water. Leaning on her knees, she lets her head dangle, enjoying the sensation of the cool plastic seat on the back of her thighs. Ylsa has been in here quite a while now. Maybe she has a bad stomach from the stress? Over the faulty tap, Zaina can hear a faint rustling, so perhaps Ylsa's on her way out. Zaina is finished too. Getting up, she pulls up her knickers and trousers, then waits for Ylsa's flush to sound so they don't cross paths.

Nothing happens for a while, and then there *is* a sound, but it's not the one Zaina's expecting. Instead of the churn of the flush she hears a quiet clanking followed by a scraping noise.

A moment later the cubicle door creaks open and there are rapid footsteps across the lino floor. The bathroom door opens with a sound of rushing air, then bangs shut, and the footsteps go rattling away down the corridor.

Zaina frowns and lets herself out of the cubicle.

It's as she's washing her hands that it occurs to her what the sound might have been.

The toilet cisterns are enclosed in wooden boxes. If you were to prise the lid off one of these boxes you would have access to the cistern. Could the scraping sound have been the replacement of this lid? And if so, was the clanking Ylsa lifting off the top of the cistern?

Shaking her hands dry she heads for the cubicle Ylsa vacated. There's no sign that the toilet has been recently used – the blue fluid the cleaners swirl round them last thing at night is still in the toilet bowl – so what was she doing in here all that time?

There are some dark scrape marks on the walls either side of the box. That could have been where the maintenance staff have gained access for plumbing purposes, but Zaina can't ignore a nagging suspicion. What if Ylsa has hidden something here to consult when she got stuck? Her phone maybe. Zaina can't risk letting her get away with that. It could be the difference between winning or missing out on the maths prize.

She hooks her fingers beneath the upper panel and it comes away surprisingly easily, revealing the white porcelain cistern beneath. Leaning the panel against the cubicle wall, she removes the heavy cistern lid and peers inside. Her heart jolts.

A resealable plastic food bag bobs on top of the water.

Inside is a folded sheet of paper.

She lays the cistern lid beside the panel and lifts the bag out. Dripping water all over her shirt, she slides open the plastic fastener and draws out the paper.

Written in blue biro on the left-hand side are numbers one to twenty-four. Beside them is a second set of numbers. These are more random, but she recognizes the first ten. They are the solutions to the exam questions she's already completed.

The sheet contains the answers to the entire paper.

Her face flashes hot with fury and her heart sets up an urgent pounding.

Zaina must report Ylsa to Mr Peters straight away and have her kicked out of the exam.

Pocketing the paper, she hurries out of the bathroom and sets off down the corridor. But as she passes the urinals the door flies open and, before she can register what is happening, she is dragged inside. Spinning her round, Nero positions himself in front of it, blocking her escape route.

"For fuck's sake, let me go! Ylsa's been cheating!"

"That doesn't matter. Listen to me."

"It *doesn't matter*!" She gives a bark of laughter. "What planet are you on?"

"Listen—"

"No! I've got an exam to finish. I care about my future even if you don't, so, no, I'm not going to listen to any more of your bullshit apologies." She makes a grab for his arm to wrench him out of her way, but he shakes her off.

"This isn't about the party. It's about Chanelle."

"Chanelle? I don't give a shit about Chanelle! If she can't be bothered to turn up for her own exam, that is not my problem!"

"Please, Zaina, just listen."

"Or what? You won't let me go?"

"Of course I will, but, please, just hear me out."

Against her will, she does.

"Something bad has happened to her," he says. "I know it. Her bag's in school, so where is she? I thought she might be in the girls' toilets, but you've just been in and she wasn't there, right? We need to find her!"

She stares at him, open-mouthed, then gathers her wits. "Are you kidding me?"

This time she's rougher with him, shoving him bodily aside; if he wants to make her stay, he'll have to resort to physical violence. As she yanks open the door, he makes a half-hearted attempt to grab at her blazer, but when she easily shakes him off, he doesn't try to stop her going back out into the corridor.

"Zai!"

She keeps walking, back towards the exam hall.

"Zaina! You don't even care that one of your friends could be bleeding out somewhere?"

She spins round. "*Bleeding out?* What are you even on? So she can't take exam pressure. Not my problem."

Nero is shaking his head. "Get your priorities right, Zaina."

"Oh, so now you're the arbiter of right and wrong?"

They stare at each other down the length of the corridor, chests heaving. The expression on his face

83

reminds her of the way he looked when she walked into that room a month ago.

"No," she says softly. "I didn't think so."

She turns round and marches away, refusing to feel guilty. Chanelle really *isn't* her problem. And anyway, she probably just went home. More important by far is the fact that Ylsa has been cheating.

But as Zaina approaches the door to the exam hall, she realizes something that makes her blood run cold. She's now seen the answers to the exam too, so it won't just be Ylsa who has her paper cancelled. And Zaina has been doing so well up to now; the sheet confirmed it. So far she's got all the answers correct.

She swears under her breath. *Fuck, fuck, fuck.*

But wait.

Is it even possible that Ylsa could have memorized every single answer?

Surely not. Plus, she won't be able to show any workings, which will be hugely suspicious if she ends up getting all the answers right. That means she'll have to get some wrong or risk disqualification, so if Zaina manages to get them all right, she'll still beat her.

Turning on her heel, she runs back to the bathroom,

prepared to punch Nero if he tries to delay her. Fortunately he's now nowhere to be seen. Hurrying into the cubicle, she replaces the paper in the bag, seals it and drops it into the cistern, then replaces the lid of the cistern and the wooden panel. She can decide later if she wants to report Ylsa.

By the time she gets back to her desk she's hotter than ever, her shirt sticking to her skin, her scalp crawling with beads of sweat. She's about to sit down when she feels a gaze on her. She glances up. Ylsa has turned round in her seat and, over the bent heads of the students in between, she's fixing Zaina with narrowed red-rimmed eyes. Momentarily their gazes are locked, and then the other girl turns away. Zaina experiences a shiver of unease. Ylsa is not someone you want to get on the wrong side of, and if she's guessed that Zaina knows she's been cheating, what will she be prepared to do to stop her from telling?

The Party

Emily Blackwater lived in a nice part of town, where the houses were not subdivided into flats and the front lawns were filled with flowers and bird feeders instead of old mattresses and Domino's boxes. Her red-bricked Victorian townhouse stood in the middle of the street, blaring K-pop and frosted with fairy lights: a gingerbread cottage guaranteed to be irresistible to any passing teenager.

As Zaina approached, her heart was drumming almost painfully and she had to take some deep breaths to prevent her apprehension from tipping over into a full-blown panic attack. The prospect of crossing the threshold felt like straying into the habitat of a different and possibly dangerous species, a species that inhabited a completely different environment, breathing air in the sunshine, while she dwelt in the twilight zone, leagues of dark water pressing down on her head.

Rolling out her shoulders, she experimented with a smile, massaging her cheeks to loosen out the stiff muscles, then she opened the wrought-iron gate and walked up the path to the front door. A silver banner had been slung across it, spelling out PARTY TIME! in rainbow letters. Her reflection wavered dimly in its mirrored surface, flickering in and out of existence as it shifted in the evening breeze.

Through the closed curtains she could make out the silhouettes of people dancing. Judging by the height and swinging asymmetric hair, one was Emily herself. In which case the others were her hot-girl friends. Zaina's dad always dismissed the popular kids, the ones with a social life they were sacrificing their future prospects for, but being young wasn't like it had been for him. The popular gang weren't all destined for hairdressing and hospitality; they didn't all get wasted on drink and drugs. Emily herself was going on to study engineering and her best friend was already making money as a music producer.

The prospect of sitting in Emily's living room trying to make shouty small talk with someone she hardly knew made her heart sink. The only thing of note that had happened to her, other than revision, in the past six months, was the death of her dad. Hardly conducive to sparkling conversation.

This was a mistake. She should just go.

The door opened and three people stumbled out, laughing: Yolanda and Bradley from her form, and, draped over Yolanda's shoulders, Poppy.

Oblivious to Zaina's presence, the group stumbled over to the hedge dividing Emily's garden from her neighbour's and Bradley set about rolling a joint. Zaina felt such a strong pang of jealousy she almost turned round and walked back out of the garden, then she saw that Poppy's apparent affection for Yolanda was just because she was too drunk to stand up on her own. At that moment her eyes rolled in Zaina's direction and swam into focus. Her expression changed.

"ZAAAAAAIIIIIIIII!" Poppy jettisoned Yolanda and came stumbling over to throw herself into Zaina's arms. "You caaaaaaaaame! Oh my God, I'm sooooooo happy!"

OK, Poppy's effusiveness might be partly down to alcohol, but it was still nice.

"Oh my days, it's the bride of Dracula," drawled Bradley. "Have you come to suck our blood?"

Zaina forced a smile as Poppy led her over to the hedge, where Yolanda air-kissed her on both cheeks and complimented her shoes.

She was grateful when the other two then resumed the conversation they'd been in the middle of, about how Saff Jackson had quit the football team. Bradley was saying it was the right thing for Saff to do as the team was for boys, not for enbies, and Saff would put them at a disadvantage, but Yolanda said Saff was more ripped than the rest of the team combined and had every right to be there.

"Were people having a go?"

Bradley shrugged, licking the edge of the large Rizla. "Not as far as I know. I think the rest of the team's pissed off, actually, as Saff's an insane tackler."

He raised the fat roll-up to his mouth and lit up. The earthy perfume of the weed filled the air. Poppy was babbling in Zaina's ear about somebody getting off with somebody else. Zaina made a sound of surprise, having no real clue how to respond to this. It was as if, during the long months of her dad's illness, she had forgotten how to speak the language of other teenagers. She could answer questions, but she had no idea what to say to them in the stretching silences that, presumably, she had once filled with inanities like this. Fortunately Poppy was too drunk to notice that the conversation was entirely one-way.

The joint appeared in front of Zaina.

She was about to refuse it, then hesitated. Her dad would never even have thought of making her promise not to take drugs, because it was such a no-brainer, but a non-promise was a non-promise and she could really do with something to ease the tension that was making her whole body ache. Accepting the joint, she took a drag, sucking the hot smoke into her lungs, determined to suffocate before she succumbed to the humiliation of coughing.

She was gratified by the glances of respect from Bradley and Yolanda when she exhaled smoothly and passed the joint back. Then she felt stupid. Her dad hadn't made her promise because he trusted her not to be so foolish. One of his friend's brothers had developed schizophrenia from smoking too much skunk. What was the point of getting straight-A stars if you couldn't work because you were hearing voices telling you to kill yourself? Yes, it was unlikely, statistically, but why take the risk?

The urge to turn round and walk back out of the gate was almost overwhelming, but if she did, she would immediately turn into gossip fodder. *Zaina Abbour had a meltdown.* Better to stay long enough that nobody would comment when she did slip away. It was pointless trying to speak to paralytic Poppy. She needed to find Nero.

"Just going to the bathroom," she muttered, but Poppy was too busy laughing like a drain at something Bradley was saying to notice.

On the way into the house she rebuked herself for her jealousy. Just because Zaina had wilfully turned herself into a hermit didn't mean Poppy had to practise purdah too. What right did Zaina have to resent her friend for carrying on with her life? It wasn't Poppy's dad who died; Poppy had made no one any promises, and she was easily on track for the grades she need to study economics at Sheffield. She was at liberty to hang out whenever she wanted and with whomever she wanted, and if that meant making new friends to replace the one who had, essentially, abandoned her, then who could blame her?

After the exams she would make more of an effort with Poppy. Aside from the fact that she was one of Zaina's absolute favourite people, Poppy had really tried to be there for her when her dad was ill. She took the 3 a.m. phone calls when Zaina needed to talk, tried to say the right things, bought gifts she clearly hoped would make Zaina feel better – bath salts and hand cream and lavender candles – but she didn't really understand because she had never lost anyone. Nero's granny had died last year, and they had been really close; it wasn't the same, but he seemed to get it.

She felt a sudden yearning to be with him, but even as she got out her phone to message him, there he was.

It was a pure Pavlovian response. Her whole body relaxed, even muscles she didn't even know were tense: those in her throat and her cheeks and her wrists. He was in the dining area at the back of the living room, talking to the football crowd, having a laugh with boys he had almost nothing in common with: the party stalwarts who got trashed every Friday and Saturday nights, who were obsessed with labels and trainers, who went to clothes drops and liked rap.

Nero liked The Smiths.

She paused in the doorway, reluctant to butt into the all-male group. Even Saff wasn't there. With their peroxide crop and multiple piercings, Saff always stood out, and normally they would be right in the middle of it all, swearing and guffawing with the rest of the team. Now Zaina spotted Saff sitting on the sofa, looking about as miserable as Zaina felt. Chanelle was sitting beside them. Chanelle was no particular favourite of Zaina's, especially now that the exams were coming up and their frenemy rivalry had broken out into open hostility, but the look of unhappiness on Chanelle's face made Zaina feel almost sorry for her. Was Saff regretting quitting the football team? If so, why had they done it? Raising the can of cider, Saff glugged it down, then crushed the can and tossed it on the carpet. Chanelle said something Zaina couldn't hear over the music and Saff rolled their eyes, got up and walked away.

Chanelle glanced self-consciously around the room to see if anyone had noticed the exchange, and Zaina didn't look away in time. Their eyes met, and in that moment raw pain was visible in Chanelle's gaze, the pain of whatever had just happened added to the shame of knowing someone had seen it and was either pitying or laughing at her. Chanelle's expression changed abruptly. Jutting out her chin she glared accusingly at Zaina. *What are you looking at?*

Zaina turned away and Nero was standing in front of her.

He had left the footballers downing shots to loyally endure his boring, miserable, monosyllabic friend. And yet the weariness he must have been feeling at the prospect of having to babysit her all night was perfectly disguised. He actually looked pleased to see her.

"Well, well. If it isn't Miss Abbour."

"Don't" – she grimaced – "I shouldn't have come."

"Course you should. Lemme get you a vodka cranberry."

She trailed him like a duckling to the kitchen, which looked like it had been raided by the police or a band of particularly destructive burglars. Every surface was covered with empty and overturned bottles, spilling their dregs on to a floor carpeted with Doritos. Soggy cigarettes floated in lager puddles, and pizza crusts lay abandoned like enormous pale grubs. The place smelled of wet tobacco and beer.

Crossing the room, Nero opened the door of the washing machine and retrieved an uncracked bottle of Smirnoff and a carton of cranberry juice. "Brought these in case you came. Didn't want anyone else getting their greasy mitts on them."

Rinsing out two abandoned glasses, he poured out the drinks and cleared a space on the worktop, drying it with the frayed sleeve of his sweatshirt. They sat down on chrome bar stools and clinked glasses.

As they drank, it transpired that she didn't have to think of any small talk after all, that it felt perfectly comfortable and not remotely awkward to sit with him in complete silence but for the heartbeat of the music in the room next door. But was Nero as comfortable? He was frowning down at his hands and biting his lip, as if he wanted to say something but didn't know how to begin. Her heart leapfrogged into her mouth. Had he started seeing someone? It wouldn't exactly have been surprising. With his tumble of black curls and beautiful eyes, he attracted a lot of attention from the type of girl who wasn't into the overly groomed good looks of some of the other boys. In Year Twelve he'd been skinny, but now he had filled out, his muscles growing into the frame of his bones, making his T-shirt drape over bumps and curves that hadn't been there before.

A gaggle of girls came in, squawking about some poor kid's dance moves.

Zaina's back straightened. These were Ylsa's friends. They were all attractive, rich and overconfident. She prepared herself for faux friendliness and bitchy smiles. But Ylsa wasn't with them.

Come to think of it, she hadn't seen Ylsa hanging out with her friend group as much recently. Mostly, when they encountered one another these days, Ylsa would be tapping into her phone and Zaina could safely ignore her.

It took a microsecond for the girls to spot the full bottle of vodka. They lunged at it, snatching it off the table.

"Sorry, ladies!" Nero said, grinning. "That's ours!"

Mela pressed the bottle between her breasts and tilted her head coyly. "You don't mind, do you Zarina?"

Zarina? Seriously? Had she been off the scene that long?

"It's fine," she said.

"Hand it over, please." Nero beckoned good-naturedly at Mela, but Zaina could see by the slight dimple in his left eyebrow that he was getting annoyed. That had also been the prelude to Nero getting a hospital security guard up against a wall when he tried to prevent them from visiting her dad's ward after hours.

Mela bent at the waist and pouted her collagen-enhanced lips at him. "Make me."

His hand shot forward and whipped the bottle out of her grasp.

Mela gasped, straightening rapidly. "Jesus!"

"Get your hands off her!" cried one of the girls.

"My hands aren't on her," Nero said coldly. "They're on our vodka."

"That was an assault," another girl said, scandalized. "You should report him."

"It's OK," Mela crooned. "Poor ickle povvo can't afford to buy another one. Let's see if there's anything left in the fridge."

As they clip-clopped across the tiles, dislike made Zaina's fists ball at her sides. She wanted to retort, *Give it five years and his company's algorithm will be sending your CV straight to trash*. Because, out of all of them, Nero would be the one to make something of himself. She had never met anyone more passionate and dedicated to the things that were important to him. He only got lower grades than hers because academic work wasn't his thing. He planned to start his own gaming company. He'd told her this, his eyes shining, during one of the interminable vigils at the hospital, showed her his notebook filled with ideas for worlds peopled by treacherous sorcerers and the heirs to poisoned thrones. She knew he would make it because he was filled with love for what he did. It was when you had no passion, only fear, that you ended up grinding through the work as she, Chanelle and Ylsa had to.

"Let's go outside," he murmured, and she got up and followed him to the glass doors that opened on to a patio where hurricane lanterns cast a romantic glow over a few abandoned glasses and stubbed-out cigarettes. But this early in the year it was too cold to linger outside for long and no other partygoers were there.

Nero sank down into a steamer chair, raised the bottle to his lips and swigged for a long time. "Jesus," he said, finally lowering the bottle. "That was not a good start."

"A good start to what?" she said, leaning on the table. She noticed he had just reduced the contents by a third.

He shrugged and smiled. "Talking. Us."

"Oka–a–ay." Her mouth was suddenly dry.

"Fuck, fuck, fuck." He swigged again.

"Without wishing to womansplain, maybe slow down?"

He gave her a mirthless smile. "Dutch courage."

So it was definite, then. He had a girlfriend and he wanted to break it to her gently because it would probably mean the end of their closeness.

Then another possibility struck her. Maybe it was worse than that. Maybe he was moving away. His dad worked on oil rigs and there had been talk of a move to Scotland, where a lot of his family lived.

He still wasn't saying anything, and his tanned skin had an unusually queasy pallor.

Oh God, he wasn't ill, was he? Boys his age could get testicular cancer, couldn't they? The muscles round her chest clamped tight, until she could only take tiny sips of breath. "Can you please tell me what is going on?" she managed hoarsely.

He got to his feet, abandoning the bottle he had fought so hard to hang on to. "Not here. Let's go somewhere more private."

More private than a deserted patio? From inside, the French doors would be a black mirror. They wouldn't be seen or heard – was that not privacy enough? Filled with apprehension, she followed him up a set of limestone steps to a brick path that led away into the shadows. As they passed flower beds already coming into bloom, her legs brushed white star-shaped flowers, releasing a delicate jasmine perfume. Up ahead she could make out the dim shape of some kind of pergola or summer house.

She caught her breath. Two small white discs glinted from the darkness.

"It's only a fox," Nero murmured. They watched each other for a few more seconds, then the eyes winked out. There was a quiet rustle and then silence.

Nero took her hand. "Come on."

By the time they reached the pergola her eyes had adjusted to the vestiges of light that reached from the house. It was a pretty little wooden construction draped in some kind of trailing plant whose runners coiled lovingly round the pillars holding up the roof. At the base of the pillars were large terracotta planters filled with lavender just coming into bud. How lovely to have a garden like this, or any garden at all. Their own flat was seven floors up, and by the latter stages of her dad's illness he'd been unable to leave, except by stretcher.

Against the wall that separated this garden from the one

behind was a bench, but she didn't feel like sitting down. She wanted to know what all this was about.

Nero didn't seem to be in a hurry to enlighten her. He leaned against a pillar with his hands in his pockets, gazing up at the moon resting on the apex of Emily's roof. It was a waning crescent (her dad had taught her how to tell), a sliver of yellow white like a nail paring. By tomorrow it would be hidden in shadow, but tonight it was beautiful.

"Christ, I could do with a fag," he muttered.

In the house beyond the path the rap music suddenly cut off and an unexpected silence fell. It felt loaded somehow, as if the whole house was holding its breath. And then the first fragile piano notes of her favourite song started up.

"*She'd take the world off my shoulders,*" crooned the singer, "*if it was ever hard to move.*"

Even with the tension of expectation, her body melted a little. The song had been everywhere before her dad got ill, so it held only good associations.

Nero turned and smiled at her and for a moment she wanted time to stop – right here in this jasmine-scented garden under the crescent moon, with her best friend beside her, listening to the song that made her heart swell.

Then he broke the spell. "What are you thinking about?"

102

She shrugged. "Nothing much. What are *you*?"

"I was thinking about the first time we met." He smiled. "I thought you were totally fantastic."

Her heart shrank down to its normal size, maybe a bit smaller. *Then as I got to know you I realized how much of a downer you are.* Was he just going to break off the friendship? Had she put him through too much with all the crying and late-night summonses?

"And then, we started hanging out more, and I realized my first impressions were completely on the money. You *are* fantastic. I'm not going to, like, list why, but—"

She forced a laugh. "List away." *I need it.*

"I don't know. You are just…" He opened his arms as if presenting her to an audience.

"So articulate. Thought you were supposed to be a hotshot at English."

"All the usual stuff, right? Clever, funny, kind, attractive."

She snorted. "I'm not kind. In fact, I'm not any of those things."

"OK, well, whatever. Your unkind, unattractive, unclever unfunniness and mine sort of click together, don't you think?"

She shrugged.

"It's been so hard for you, with your dad, but it will get better. I know it will. And I want to be beside you when the sun comes out again, when it's shining full in our faces and our shadows are behind us."

Her breath caught. Maybe he wasn't so bad at English after all.

The breeze stiffened, snatching away the jasmine perfume and replacing it with something more pungent and animal. Perhaps the fox had marked its territory. Was it still watching them? She shivered, drawing her jacket round her shoulders and peering anxiously into the shadows.

"Zaina?"

He had moved closer to her and his gold-flecked eyes were fixed on hers. "You know how much I like you, right? As a friend, of course, but" – he took a deep breath – "more than that too."

She froze.

"And … and, well, I think you feel the same. Do you? Do you feel that way about me, Zai?"

She couldn't breathe. Couldn't speak. He was looking at her with wide-open eyes and the dimple had gone from his eyebrow. And now he was leaning in, and his soft lips were touching hers and she was rooted to the spot and couldn't move—

Until she could.

He stumbled back, coming up sharply against the pergola support and almost losing his balance. He blinked rapidly, like a child unexpectedly bitten by the dog he had tried to pet.

She looked down at the hands that had shoved him away. The ink-stained, pasty hands that had held her father's yellow claw and promised not to let him down, to let nothing distract her from reaching her full potential, from becoming what he had failed to become.

Rage surged up from her belly like lava. Nero knew full well what her dad had said, the promise she had made. "What the hell is wrong with you?"

"I…" he stammered.

"I literally just lost my dad, I've got my A-levels in a month, and now you lay this on me?"

He swayed slightly as he stared at her, his eyes round.

"You want to do all that trivial shit, kissing and blow jobs and fucking and whatever else boys seem to think is so damn important, go get yourself a girlfriend in there."

She swept an angry arm towards the glowing house that seemed so very far away. "Because I am totally not interested. In fact, I'm angry that you even thought I would be."

"Angry?" he breathed.

"You clearly don't know me at all – what I've been through—"

"Angry?" he said again in a stronger voice. "I was there with you the whole time your dad was dying."

"Oh, what, and so now I have to sleep with you to pay you back?"

He blanched. "What? What did you just say?"

But she couldn't repeat the monstrous insult. She couldn't utter another word because something other than rage was now surging up from her stomach.

His eyes glinted as if they were made of dark glass that had shattered into splinters. He took a deep inhalation, like someone close to drowning who had finally broken the surface of the water. "I'm so very fucking sorry, Zaina. I can promise you I will never make such an incredibly infuriating mistake again."

As he stalked away, up the garden, the lights from the house threw out his long shadow behind him, so long that it stretched all the way to where she was standing, like a black shroud laid over her. He opened one of the French doors and there was a sudden blast of rap music, and then it closed and he was gone.

She turned round and vomited vodka and cranberry into the lavender planter.

The Exam

9:00–9:15

Zaina sits back down. She's spent so much time in this bloody chair over the past few weeks it almost feels as if her spine is moulded to the shape of the plastic. Her pen lies on the open page of the exam paper, the last part of the inscription facing up: *Daddy.* She can't quite bring herself to pick it up.

This is the hard bit of an exam – when the adrenaline has worn off and you're tired and your brain hurts. The part where you just have to grind through.

And she will. In a minute.

Sighing, she looks out of the window.

Only the roof of the science block, flat and featureless

but for a half-deflated football, lies between her and the cloudless horizon. Of course, beyond the science block are more buildings – shops and apartments and office blocks – hundreds of roofs that Zaina imagines hurdling to reach the perfect blue sky. But, in reality, you'd never get there. You'd just keep running as the earth rolled beneath you, like a hamster on a wheel, trying to get to somewhere that was always just out of reach.

She looks down at her pen.

After this exam everyone will be celebrating the fact that it's all over, but it's never really over, because then comes university, then finding your first job, then trying to climb up the greasy pole to more senior positions. And if, by some miracle, you make it all the way to the top you have to try and stay there. An exhausted, terrified hamster scampering on the wheel for ever.

She sighs. When are you allowed to stop and look around you? Just kick your legs and watch the clouds go by? Never. Or at least people like her aren't. Maybe it's possible for the ones born with a silver spoon in their mouth, like Ylsa, who can take a gap year, or screw up her exams and retake them – the parachute will always be there. But normal people just have to keep striving and striving until they die. Though at least if you work hard from the beginning you get a decent wage and then there are other things to mitigate the drudgery: nice cars and holidays, a house with a garden, meals out. Little treats you exchange for your precious limited time. But if you waste the opportunities you're offered when you're young, there's no going back; you'll work just as hard, if not harder, but in a less well-paid job. Better to sacrifice your happiness now for the long-term gain. That's what her dad said. As his last hours and minutes and seconds trickled through his fingers.

Still she can't bring herself to pick up her pen. She wants to but her body won't obey. The little notch in her finger aches dully. The air in the room has congealed, as if they're all preserved in aspic, hunched over their desks like they will be for the rest of their lives, with only the layout of the furniture changing. *Education will set you free*, her dad liked to say, but what if it doesn't? What if it just makes the trappings of your cage more attractive?

She tries to recall the last time she felt happy, and it comes to her almost straight away.

Standing in the doorway of a party she didn't want to be at, with music she hated and people she couldn't be bothered to talk to, and then seeing Nero across the room, and him looking up and seeing her.

She has a powerful urge to just get up and leave, hurl her paper in the air and walk out, leaving everything and everyone behind her, and just keep walking towards that freedom beyond the science-block roof.

But she can't. Because, whether she likes it or not, her dad is right.

With one last longing look at the solitary football sunning itself under the blue sky, she settles back down to work.

Question eleven.

It's a graph question. Piece of piss.

She slogs through the calculations, fills in the table and finally starts to plot them on the graph paper they have been given.

One of the points doesn't fit on the line of best fit. *Bloody bollocking shit*. She's made a miscalculation somewhere in the process and now she's going to have to go back and recheck the whole damn thing.

But as she's poring over the numbers she becomes aware of a scratching noise coming from a few desks down.

It takes a moment for Zaina to work out that the noise

is Saff's silver wristband scraping against the desk, and that this is caused by the shaking of their hand.

Zaina frowns. The noise is annoying and distracting, but hardly something she could complain about without looking like a dick; if it's down to nerves, there's nothing Saff or Mr Peters could do about it. But it's not like Saff to be nervous. Zaina can remember overhearing Chanelle bragging about the amazing penalty Saff had scored in the ninety-third minute of a match, snatching the victory. And yet now Saff's entire plaid shirt is wet with sweat and clinging to their muscular back. Yes, it's hot in here, but not that hot.

Zaina jumps as Mr Peters passes close to her desk and heads over to Nero's.

Her heart sinks as she watches him gather up Nero's paper and carry it, along with his pencil case and water bottle, back to the invigilator's desk. That's it. He's been disqualified.

Nero, you fucking moron.

For some reason she feels like crying. Not least because she's double-checked all her calculations for question eleven and they all seem correct. They *have* to be. What is she not seeing?

Then she spots the final part of the question: *Suggest a reason for the outlying point on the x axis.*

She swears so loudly that Mr Peters looks sharply at her.

Her heart starts pounding. All that time wasted because she didn't read the question properly.

She glances at the clock. It's almost nine fifteen. They are almost midway through the exam and she is only just halfway through the paper. The last half is going to get much harder, and now she won't have time to go and check through anything. Though at least she knows that the first ten answers are correct.

Can she really just ignore the fact that Ylsa had the answers? What would her dad tell her to do?

Not to worry about what anyone else was doing, to concentrate on her own business. Be the best she can be.

Going back to the paper, she sets about tackling the next question. But she is not allowed to concentrate for long. Gradually she becomes aware that someone, somewhere very far away, is playing the piano. At first she thinks it must be someone practising in the music rooms at the other end of the building, but there's no way she'd be able to hear that from here. It sounds both close and far at the same time. She frowns, straining to pick out the sound over the ambient noise of the exam room, because there's something familiar about the melody taking shape at the very edge of her hearing.

Her breath catches.

"Glimpse of Us". Her favourite song.

It has a tinny quality. She glances around the room to see if anyone else has noticed. If someone's smuggled their phone in here, they will be in big trouble.

Nobody else has looked up. She turns her head a fraction – is it coming from the desk on the other side of Nero's? No. She leans forward slightly; is it the girl in front of her? Nope.

She sits back and the sound doesn't change in volume.

The song is on her playlist, but she definitely left her phone in her bag in the locker.

Didn't she?

She breaks out in a cold sweat. What if she didn't? What if she accidentally brought it in here? Surely she would have noticed before now. It would have bumped against her side when she went to the toilets. But she needs to make sure. With her eyes fixed on Mr Peters, she slides her hands into her pockets.

She exhales. Nothing.

Wait. Not quite nothing. Tucked into the corner of the left-hand pocket is something small and hard. A throat lozenge from when she last had Covid? But it's not wrapped in paper, so why isn't it sticky? She runs her fingertips over the smooth, curved surface and her heart plummets off the edge of a cliff.

The terrible truth is confirmed when she clamps her hand round it and the music becomes muffled.

Someone has slipped an AirPod into her pocket.

She glances around in panic, but thankfully no one seems to have noticed.

The music buzzes against her palm, rising in volume.

What the actual fuck? Whose AirPod is this and why is it in her pocket? Chanelle? Realizing she's blown her own chances, is she trying to screw up Zaina's too?

She has to tell Mr Peters. What other choice does she have? If she takes her hand away from the speaker, someone might notice and then what? Having a Bluetooth device in your pocket during your A-level maths exam isn't a good look. Mr Peters is a few rows down, crouching beside Ylsa's desk, murmuring quietly to her while Ylsa nods, her head bent miserably.

Zaina puts up her right hand and waits for him to notice her. Then from the corner of her eye she becomes aware that she is not the only one whose attention is fixed on Ylsa's desk. The new girl, Tabitha, is looking across at Ylsa with an expression of pure loathing. It's so intense that Zaina is taken aback. Whatever happened between them at the party must have been a big deal.

Evidently Tabitha feels Zaina's gaze because her head turns and their eyes meet.

Zaina snaps her head down to her paper. *What is going on here?* She hardly knows Tabitha at all, but what possible reason could the new girl have for hating Ylsa? Is she too after the maths prize? That feels like an oddly trivial reason for the degree of hatred she was directing towards Ylsa.

But if so, does Tabitha hate her too? And Chanelle?

Could the new girl have something to do with the AirPod? Or Chanelle's no-show?

Stop, she commands her runaway mind. *Just stop. Whatever beef Tabitha has with Ylsa, and whatever the reason for Chanelle's disappearance, they are none of your business.* Hearing footsteps, she glances up to see that Mr Peters is walking away from Ylsa's desk. She is about to put her hand up again when she realizes that the music has stopped. Tentatively she lets go of the AirPod and wipes her sweaty hand on her trousers. Maybe the sweat affected the electronics.

Then she frowns. There aren't many people who know "Glimpse of Us" is her favourite song. Only two, in fact, and one of them is furiously scribbling on her paper three rows up from Zaina, her highlighted head bent in concentration. The other is— Ah.

Nero must have slipped the AirPod into her pocket after he dragged her into the toilet. That moment he made a half-hearted grab for her blazer, he was dropping it in. He knew the Joji song was her favourite and he was playing it at full volume to remind her of the party, to try to upset her and throw her off her game. And it almost works, as the memory comes, unbidden, to her mind, of how he looked when he walked away from the pergola back to the party, twisting her heart so hard it takes her breath away. But then she remembers what happened afterwards and the tears dry up. She has absolutely nothing to feel guilty for.

She fills in the next answer with such force the pen nib cuts all the way through the paper, then she moves on to the next, jabbing figures savagely into her calculator.

Someone says her name.

She freezes.

Even tinny, distorted and barely audible, she knows that voice by heart. She is about to take the AirPod out of her pocket and surreptitiously crush it under her shoe when there is movement in her peripheral vision.

She glances out of the window. Nero is standing on the roof of the science block, staring in at her, while holding his phone to his mouth.

"Zaina," says the AirPod, "you need to listen."

The Party

She stayed where she was for a long time, hunched on the garden bench in the darkness, hugging her knees to her abdomen and rocking back and forth in an attempt to keep warm. It wasn't even that cold, but she was shivering so hard her teeth chattered.

How could he do that to her, knowing what she had been through? How could he spoil the one thing she thought she could rely on when everything else was changing? The friendship she had come to value even more than Poppy's, because it had seemed so unconditional.

But there *was* a condition. Of course there was. He was

like every other member of the male species. They couldn't just be your friend, couldn't see the value in that kind of love. The only kind they valued was the kind involving their dicks. She knew a hundred boys who had looked into their girlfriends' eyes and told them they loved them, just to get the girls to put out. It had happened to Poppy last year. She had lost her virginity to some shithead who forwarded topless pictures of her to his friends and was almost expelled for it.

Boys are only after one thing. Her dad had told her that too. *I know. I was one.*

How could she have been naive enough to think that Nero was different from the football orcs he got on with so well? He could fit in with every friendship group because he always knew the right thing to say to twist people round his finger. That wasn't charisma; it was manipulation. And he had manipulated her just the same.

The realization was like a gut punch: the friendship she had clung to like a life raft over the past six months wasn't even real. All that time she was looking into his eyes and trusting him with her deepest fears and sorrows, he was trying to work out how long he had to put up with this before he could get into her knickers.

And now it was over.

You were right, Daddy.

Eventually her breathing settled and she found the strength to get to her feet. As she limped up the brick path towards the house, she could smell the earthy aroma of weed. Poppy must be out of her mind by now. She felt a stirring of guilt. It had been obvious when she arrived that Poppy was off her head, but Zaina hadn't stayed with her and hadn't tried to stop her smoking the joint. A real friend would have done that.

There had been times over the past few months when, in comparison with Nero's apparent devotion, Poppy's friendship had seemed lacking, but now she understood: Nero was only investing the time because of what he hoped he could get out of it. Poppy had checked in every day, but she had her own life, other friends, boyfriends. Hadn't she just split up with someone? Zaina should know that. Yes, her dad had died, but other people were going through stuff too. It was time she put some work into a friendship that was actually real.

But not now. Right now she just wanted to go home and go to bed. Not that she'd sleep. Nero hadn't just ruined her evening and screwed up the next few weeks (months?)

as she tried to get over this; he had probably messed up her revision too. How would she concentrate now? She was going to let her dad down over the very thing he had specifically warned her against.

The boys were back in charge of the music and as she opened the French doors she was smacked in the face by drill. The kitchen was busier now. The less popular kids, clearly exhausted from their clumsy attempts at socializing, had gathered there in defensive little huddles, muttering to one another and chuckling self-consciously, relieved, perhaps, to be able to speak naturally again without the pressure of being cool or funny. They were probably happy to have been invited but would be even happier once it was all over.

"Hi, Zaina," said the diminutive Jasper Oates, standing with his usual clump of oddballs. "Fancy a drink?"

Mind-blowingly good at ping-pong and chess, Jasper had already been accepted to study classics at Oxford. Because of Zaina's maths results, he clearly had her down as a fellow neek.

"I think I'm going to head off, actually," she said, smiling wanly.

"You don't know what you're missing," Jasper, said with

a wink, as his oddball friends stared, speechless with shock at one of their own actually flirting with a female. "I'm an expert at the fianchetto position."

She smiled for real this time. "Tempting, but I'm still going home."

"Are you sure? I'll be eating my queen." He raised an eyebrow.

"Goodnight, Jasper."

She left him muttering, "I knew that was too much. Gods damn it."

Her smile faded as she stepped out into the hall and saw that to get to the front door she would have to squeeze past the football team, who now lined the walls, guffawing and braying to one another as they knocked back cans of strong lager.

She had no intention of making herself the object of their attention. She just needed to hide somewhere quiet until they'd found some new territory to occupy and she could make her escape.

The living room was out. The heart of the party, this was where the sound system and drinks table were, and though she was metres from the door, she could feel the heat radiating from the room with the press of hot bodies inside. Beside her was another door, this one closed. On it was a handwritten sign reading KEEP OUT.

She had no intention of making a mess, so surely Emily wouldn't mind if she just sat there quietly for a while.

It was only as she nudged the door open a crack that she realized she wasn't the only one who had been seeking privacy. If it weren't for the volume of the music, she would certainly have heard the voices coming from the room because they were raised in anger.

Peering in, Zaina thought Saff Jackson looked out of place amid the understated elegance of the study. Standing to their full height, they dominated the room with sheer bulk, and the ferocity was coming off them in waves. Breathing strenuously through their nose, Saff's broad face was red, the grey eyes flashing as they bellowed, "You just don't fucking get it!"

It was to Chanelle's credit that she did not look scared. Her voice was calm and steady when she spoke. "I understand, Saff, I do. But it'll be fine, I promise."

"It won't be fucking fine, Chan! Honestly, I'm done, I'm finished." They spun round to the bookcases, raking their fingers through their hair.

"You are not." Chanelle walked over to her partner and placed a hand on Saff's meaty shoulder.

It all happened at once. Feeling the touch, Saff jerked away angrily, perhaps not realizing Chanelle was so close because their shoulder caught her full in the face. Chanelle staggered back, clutching her mouth. At her cry, Saff turned and they just stared at one another, both faces filled with horror. Then Saff bolted for the door.

Zaina threw herself back against the staircase as Saff wrenched the door fully open. For a moment their gazes locked and Zaina shrank from the rage and confusion burning out of Saff's eyes, then Saff reeled away down the hallway. Even the football boys were shocked into silence and simply stared after their teammate as Saff kicked open the front door and vanished into the night. There was a beat of silence, then one of the boys trilled a mocking *Whoo-oooo!* and everything carried on as before.

Chanelle straightened up and put a hand to her lip. It came away bloody. Then her head snapped up.

Zaina couldn't move.

For a split second Chanelle's expression was wide open. Her eyes were filled with distress and fear and anger: all the raging emotions she was usually able to keep in check.

127

A rivulet of blood ran down her chin from a neat split in her lip.

"Are you OK?" Zaina said.

Chanelle's eyes turned cold and as sharp as glass, and her mouth became a thin line. "I'm fine. Are *you*?"

"I just thought…"

Chanelle's face twisted in anger. "You thought what?"

Zaina sighed. "Forget it." She turned and began walking away.

"If you're looking for Poppy, by the way," Chanelle called after her, "she went upstairs."

Zaina turned back and thanked her, surprised by the unexpected friendliness, but Chanelle's expression was as stony as ever.

Zaina headed for the stairs. Poppy was too drunk to be of any use in this situation, but at least she could lie down quietly with her. They would speak properly tomorrow if she wasn't too hungover.

She was halfway up when a hand closed on her ankle. Chanelle had come out of the study and was reaching through the banisters. When she spoke, her voice was so quiet that Zaina had to strain to hear her over the music. "Go home, Zaina. Go back to your revision."

Oh yeah, *there* was the Chanelle Zaina knew.

Shaking herself free, she continued up the stairs.

At least the enmity in the drill songs was honest. She and Chanelle and Ylsa pretended to be civil when they hated each other with as much venom as the rapper, now describing his blade dripping with his rival's blood.

She arrived at the first-floor landing. It was definitely quieter up here. Doors led off the two arms of the landing, some ajar, some closed. She headed for an open door halfway down on the right-hand side. Even if Poppy wasn't there, if it was a bedroom she would lie down. She felt drained and feeble, like she'd run a marathon or was recovering from a bout of flu.

The walls of the landing were covered in photographs. There was one of Emily around Heli's age, holding a coloured windmill and sitting on the knee of a very old lady in a wheelchair. Toddler Emily was gazing adoringly at the old woman, who was gazing adoringly back, but she looked in her eighties or nineties so must surely be dead by now. Looking into baby Emily's face, Zaina pitied that innocent smiling toddler for what she had coming. There were pictures of Zaina and her dad looking at one another like that. In the years before his illness, when he thought he had a lifetime to impart the paternal advice he actually had to cram into a few short months. If he'd had a bit longer, a year or two maybe, would they have been able to simply enjoy one another's company as they used to, without the sense of dreadful urgency that characterized those last moments together? As the end approached, she'd just had to nod and listen and promise. There was no space for her to ask, to confide, to cry.

But what would she have said if she'd had the time?

I don't know what to do, Daddy.

I'm scared.

I don't want you to go.

That would only have made him feel worse about leaving them.

He had given her the pen when he knew he was dying. It had cost a ridiculous amount of money so she had to be grateful, but from the word go she was terrified of using it in case she broke the nib or lost it. And afterwards it didn't bring back happy memories because it only preserved the worst of him: all the expectation and none of the love.

She caught hold of the banister beside her.

The worst of him? How ungrateful could you get?

How disappointed he would be if he could hear her. How hurt. Her insides squirmed with guilt, turning over and over themselves like a snake trying to get out of the jaws of a mongoose. Guilt had her in its grip permanently these days, and sometimes it decided to clamp down on her. Usually out of the blue like this, when she hadn't even been thinking about him.

She concentrated on her breathing, trying to oxygenate her brain, to persuade her endocrine system not to release any more cortisol. Her breath shuddered in and out and Emily's baby face dissolved into a pink blur.

"I don't know what made you think this was any of your business."

The door up ahead was wrenched open and Ylsa strode out on to the landing.

"Fine," came a second female voice. "But I've seen the way this plays out and I don't want to watch someone else get hurt."

Fortunately Ylsa's attention was still focused on the person inside the room and Zaina had time to duck through the open door into what seemed like a guest room. It was furnished tastefully in beige and white, the

131

only ornaments a vase of dried hydrangeas and an altar candle in a wooden candlestick, but it was twice the size of her mum's bedroom. Slipping behind the door she peered through the crack. Ylsa stood stiff-backed on the landing, glaring into the room she had just stormed out of.

"Hurt? You are so wrong to the point of being delusional. The only person in danger of being hurt round here is you, so I advise you to keep your mouth shut or I will make your life very difficult."

Ylsa's chest was rising and falling very rapidly. She was a beautiful girl, there was no getting away from it (even though Poppy said that was mostly because she could afford the most expensive make-up), but as her face twisted in hatred, she looked positively ugly.

"Really?" snorted the other voice. "You're threatening me? I'm trying to help you."

"Too right I'm threatening you. Tell a single fucking soul and I will destroy you. I mean it."

And then the little rich girl, normally so confident and self-possessed, scampered across the landing and went tottering down the stairs in her high heels as if demons were after her.

Zaina shrank back into the shadows as the second figure stepped out on to the landing.

It was Tabitha.

There was something watchful about the new girl, her resting expression wary and closed off. What had she found out about Ylsa that was so frightening to the other girl? Whatever it was, Ylsa's threats didn't seem to have bothered her much. She ran a hand through her floppy fringe, then set off in the direction of the stairs. She was make-up free and wearing a baggy T-shirt over her flared jeans – decidedly underdressed for a party that most of the girls had attended in cocktail dresses and heels.

There was no love lost between Zaina and Ylsa, but as the new girl walked slowly down the stairs, Zaina felt almost sorry for Ylsa. She certainly wouldn't want Tabitha knowing any of *her* secrets.

And then halfway down the stairs, as if through some ESP, Tabitha stopped and her head turned towards the door Zaina was hiding behind. From where she stood, bathed in the party lights, the gap in the door must have been just a sliver of blackness, but the way Tabitha stared, with her expressionless dark eyes, you would have thought she could see straight through the wood.

In the gloom of the lifeless guest room, Zaina shivered. The party was well named. The *fun* seemed to have stopped for quite a few of the partygoers already tonight.

The Exam

9:15–9:30

Suddenly she's looking at Nero properly for the first time in a month. He's changed, become rangier. His edges have sharpened and his face has lost the almost feminine prettiness that made the girls describe him as "cute", which he hated. Maybe he likes this new look better: leaner, more predatory, more true to his character. His shadow stretches across the science-block roof, long in the low morning light.

Heart beating faster, she glances around the room. Every other head is bent in concentration and Mr Peters is perched on the corner of the invigilator's desk, scrolling on his phone, facing away from the window bank. No one else has seen Nero.

She turns back to the window and their eyes lock. It's been so long since she could bring herself to look at him that the act of doing so raises goosebumps across her skin.

To think she used to fall asleep in those wiry arms, rest her head against that chest. She thought she knew him down to his bones, that they were almost one person, but there were parts of him that were hidden to her. Parts that others knew better than her. The parts that made him a boy and made her a girl: the gulf between those two facts like the plummeting drop between the buildings now separating them.

Raising his right hand, he points to his ear.

She narrows her eyes.

"Zaina," buzzes the AirPod again.

She mouths *Fuck off* and looks back down at the paper. But she can't stop her treacherous eyes sliding sideways to see what he is doing.

She frowns. His arms have dropped to his sides and he is walking slowly backwards across the roof. It's a fairly narrow building, with the car park forming an L-shape around it. Another ten steps or so and he will have reached the drop on the other side. He'd better stop or he'll plummet down on to the concrete.

136

He raises his finger and points to his ear.

She shakes her head quickly. He's about five metres away from the edge of the roof. He needs to stop or he's going to fall.

But he doesn't stop.

He's not seriously going to walk off the edge of the building if she doesn't listen to what he has to say?

Three metres.

Her heartbeat speeds up.

One.

He bloody well is.

Snatching the AirPod from her pocket she stuffs it into her ear and pulls her hair down to cover it. He stops backing away, walks forward again and sits down on the asphalt. "If you can hear me, scratch your nose."

She extends her middle finger and does so.

He chuckles. "Firstly, this isn't about the party, so don't tell Mr Peters or drop my AirPod into your water bottle or anything. I do want to talk about that, but not now. I understand this exam is important to you, but there's something else going on. Something serious."

Against her will, her body responds to his voice the way it always used to. Her muscles relax so much the pen slips

137

from her hand. It only lasts a moment, then she gathers her wits again. Resting her left cheek on her hand so that she can keep looking out of the window in a plausibly natural way, she scowls at him and flips her hand palm up. *What?*

"I said this wasn't going to be about the party, but I guess it is a bit. I haven't been able to concentrate since. It really screwed with my focus, you know? My mind just kept going over and over what happened, finding a million ways to do it all differently so that we didn't end up … here."

She knows. The amount of time she's spent staring at her books, without actually taking anything in. She's done twice the number of revision hours she did for her mocks and retained half the information, which is why she needs all the thinking time she can get. It's frustrating not to be able to vent these feelings, but there's no way of responding to him; she can only listen.

"So, anyway, the first two papers didn't go well, and I was panicking. I thought I'd miss out on my Lancaster place, so … I decided to try something else."

She closes her eyes and listens to his breath. It's so familiar she can almost feel its warmth on her cheek.

"Everyone knows they keep the maths papers in Room

M1," he went on. "That's why it gets locked during exams, but I knew I could get in with one of the teacher's IDs. In case they restricted access to the maths teachers, I decided to swipe Miss Zita's."

Zaina winces. Miss Zita is head of maths, but it would take a brave person to dare to steal from her.

"I hung around yesterday after the last revision session."

Miss Zita had offered final cramming sessions before every exam, which was good of her, Zaina supposes, though she spent most of it telling them all how useless they were and how she'd never had a class more likely to fail.

"She was on her way to the car park and her bag was slung over her shoulder with her pass clipped to the strap. I ran after her and asked her all these questions and while she was droning on I just unclipped it. Classic misdirection. I wish you'd seen. You'd have been impressed."

Zaina revolves her finger. *Get on with it.*

"Anyway, then I went back into the building and waited till everyone was gone. When I was pretty sure I was alone I headed to M1. But as I turned the corner I saw that someone else had had the same idea. Zai, it was Chanelle."

Zaina frowns.

139

"She was trying to get into the maths room with a credit card or something, poking it in and out of the door jamb and jiggling it around. I didn't think she had a chance, and it didn't seem to be working, so then she crouches down and peers through the gap between the door and the door jamb. I guess trying to see what she's doing wrong. And then suddenly she stops and straightens up. She goes really still and stiff for a moment, and then she starts to turn, as if she's going to leave. Then the door opens."

Zaina glances automatically at Chanelle's empty desk. Everyone else's attention is fixed on their paper. Hardly surprising. The clock above the invigilator's desk now reads 9:23. Just over one hour left. And here she is wasting that valuable time listening to irrelevant nonsense from Nero. Mr Peters' back is turned as he walks away down the adjacent aisle, so she risks a fairly vehement hand gesture, which she hopes adequately communicates to Nero *What the hell does this have to do with me?*

"Wait," he says, "I'm getting there. So Chanelle just stands there like a rabbit in the headlights, and I realize that someone is *inside* the room, standing in the doorway. I can't see them from where I'm standing but they must have

140

heard her trying to get in. For, like, a minute Chanelle just stares, and I can hear a voice speaking to her, quietly but kind of urgently. Then she starts backing away, like she's scared."

Zaina finds herself holding her breath. He always could spin a tale.

"I know then that whoever's in the room is going to come after her, and they're gonna see me and whatever punishment she's about to get is going to come down on me too, especially if they find Zita's pass on me, so I leg it back down the corridor and out of the building. My bus is just pulling into the stop and I manage to catch it and get on. I'm feeling pretty relieved as it drives away, but when I look back, the college seems totally deserted. I can see through the windows from outside and there's no sign of Chanelle or whoever it was in the maths room, and I figure that's because she's getting a right talking-to, and I'm just glad it isn't me."

Zaina taps her middle finger on the desk impatiently. *And?*

"So, when I saw her, Chanelle had her bag with her, like she was about to go home. Now it's back in the locker room but Chanelle isn't here, and there's blood on the top pages of the papers – mine and yours. And my brain's going round and round like it did after the party, because I just can't stop thinking: what if something's happened to her, Zai?"

She stares at him. How is she supposed to respond to this?

"Her bag had all her books from the final revision session, so if she left it here, she wouldn't have been able to do any cramming last night, and if she never left, then she's somewhere in the school right now, which makes me wonder if whatever happened in M1 upset her so much she's … you know, done something. Hurt herself." He takes a deep breath. "That's why I left the exam. I'm going to look for her."

She feels a flash of jealousy for Chanelle because Nero is clearly worried about her. Then he speaks again, and this time his voice is softer. "I guess I just wanted to let you know. Because we used to talk about everything, didn't we? I know you don't want to hear this, but I'll regret what happened at the party for the rest of my life."

Her breath catches. Not again. Not now.

"It was my fault. All of it. Not Poppy's."

She gives a sharp shake of her head, though she doesn't know if he can even see it with the sun bouncing off the windows. From what Zaina glimpsed before she ran down the stairs, Poppy was taking an active and enthusiastic part in proceedings.

"I was drunk too. And I was hurt, and my pride was dented. I know that's shitty and shameful. Believe me, I hate myself for it. You deserved better after what you'd been through. You deserve better anyway, better than some drunk shithead coming on to you, then storming off when you said no, then … sleeping with your best friend."

But you *were my best friend.* A tear wells in her eye and she swipes it away savagely. *Who came on to who?* she wants to demand. She's pretty sure it must have been Poppy. She always gets amorous when she's drunk, so maybe it's to Nero's credit that he didn't seek to shift the blame.

"I just want you to know that if you can ever forgive me, I don't care how long it takes, I'll do any—"

A shadow falls across her desk. Her heart jolts. Mr Peters is standing by the window, looking out at the science-block roof. The hand holding the phone drops to Nero's side.

The Party

For what felt like a very long moment, Tabitha held her gaze through the banister rails and Zaina wondered if the new girl was going to have a go at her for listening in on a private conversation. But then Tabitha looked away without a word and descended the stairs, disappearing out of sight. Zaina exhaled. She could rest here for a while, until she was feeling better, then she should probably go looking for Poppy, check she was OK and not drowning in her own vomit or having unwise sex with some dickwad.

She was about to go over to the bed when she heard giggling.

Peering back through the gap in the door she saw two

girls from her chemistry class coming up the stairs. Her heart sank. Judging by the graphic PDA, they would be on the hunt for a bedroom. The party had clearly delivered for some, then.

As they paused halfway up the stairs to kiss, their hands all over one another, Zaina took the opportunity to slip out of the room. Since they were blocking her escape route down, she headed along the landing to a narrower staircase that led up to a further floor. Emily's house was massive. What the hell did they do with all these rooms?

As she mounted the stairs, the party lights and the music became muted. Peace at last. At the top step she sank down on the thick cream carpet, her heart scraping in her chest. The adrenaline of her fight with Nero had drained away, leaving her sick and feeble.

Through the banisters she saw the two girls pull each other into the bedroom she had just vacated and close the door.

She envied them. Not for the kissing but the sheer pleasure, they were taking in each other's company. She remembered experiencing that same joy in Nero's company in the few short months after she joined Franklyn but before her dad's diagnosis. They were always laughing, pushing each other around, chasing breathlessly after each other like children. Had she thought about his body then? Had she wanted to put her hands on it and have his hands on her? It was hard to remember because as her dad became more unwell, the human body had become something distasteful, something you tried not to think about. She'd had to force herself to ignore her father's physical appearance and focus on the human being beneath. That was the important thing. The rest was unimportant. *Trivial shit*, as she'd snarled at Nero.

It struck her then, the enormity of it. Someone (other than her family) had basically said that they loved her.

And instead of falling into his arms, she had sneered at him, dismissing his feelings as grubby and worthless.

From the bedroom on the floor below came faint murmuring and stifled laughter. She couldn't bear to listen. Getting to her feet she stepped out on to the second-floor landing.

It was quiet up here and much darker. Above her head was a skylight but the silver light from the waning moon was as fragile as gossamer. Far below, the music was a heartbeat throbbing through the floor. On the wall in front of her was a picture she could dimly make out in the gloom, a pen and ink drawing of a tree, the beautiful verdant part of it above ground, leaves basking in the sun, while the roots delved through the soil like buried bones.

She thought of the ink pen her father had given her, and experienced the flash of panic she always felt when it came to her mind. Where was it? She exhaled. Back on her desk in her bedroom where she had been revising. She should have stayed at home, then she and Nero would never have had to have that conversation. She should go home now, as Chanelle suggested.

But from down below the football boys had begun to sing, a boisterous, deep-throated bellow that competed with the bassline of the music. There would be no slipping past them now, and she really didn't want to run into Nero.

The floor seemed deserted, so Chanelle must have given her the wrong steer about Poppy being up here. No surprises there. Zaina had nothing to do now but wait for a suitable moment to make her escape.

Three doors led off the landing. One of them might be a bedroom. She felt so exhausted she might even sleep. A quick nap would refresh her for a late-night revision session.

The first door led to a bathroom. The second was a

storage room filled with plastic boxes, tents, wellington boots, suit bags, children's toys and other ephemera. She crossed to the third door, which was slightly ajar, and pushed it open.

It was too dark to see much as the curtains had been drawn across, but she sensed a larger space. She took a step inside and almost tripped over something on the floor. Perhaps this was another storage room (how lovely to have two entire rooms for random crap). She reached for the light switch, to flick it on just long enough to map out a path to the bed. But as she patted the wall for the switch, she realized the room wasn't completely quiet. She could hear breathing and rustling. The message from her brain raced to get to her hand and tell it *stop!* but it was too late. Her finger was already on the switch. The light blared on, as shocking as a scream.

In the centre of the room, marooned in a sea of abandoned clothes, was a bed.

On the bed was a tangle of limbs, hanks of dark and light hair coiled together, lips and hands and bare skin.

"Oh," she said. She was going add, *I'm sorry*. She was going to back out of the room, stepping over the trainers that had tripped her.

Nero's trainers. Next to Poppy's high heels.

But she couldn't move a muscle. Could hardly breathe.

The light shining through the wicker canes of the lampshade cast shadow scratches on the wall, as if someone had been scrabbling to get out.

Zaina had wanted time to stop in the garden, but it didn't. It stopped here, and even as the noise in her head became louder than the drill music hammering through the floorboards, she wondered if the sight of her best friends' naked entwined bodies and stunned intoxicated eyes would be all she ever saw.

MISS TABITHA JAIN

RECORDED INTERVIEW

Date: 28th June

Location: South Harrow Police Station

Time: 9:15

Conducted by officers from the Met Police

POLICE: Whenever you're ready, Miss Jain.

TJ: What do you want to know?

POLICE: Whatever you can tell us about what was going on at Franklyn Roberts Academy in the weeks prior to the events of the twenty-seventh of June. You just tell us what you know and at the end we'll ask any questions we need to.

TJ: OK. Well, I only came to Franklyn because of what happened at my last school.

They handled what that arsehole did to my friend so badly that she ended up suicidal. Not that I thought Franklyn would be any better. All schools are run by adults, aren't they, and all adults are interested in is themselves at the end of the day. Most of them don't give a shit about their students, as long as they can't be held accountable for anything that happens on their watch. So I just decided to do the same. Self-preservation. This sort of crap was never going to be my problem again. I had no interest in making friends at Franklyn. I just wanted to get through to the end and move on; leave all that *he said/she said* bullshit behind me. Looking back, I guess that was naïve. You never leave it behind, because it's human nature. People hurt each other, and when people are hurt, or angry or scared, they're dangerous.

But on my first day at the school I literally couldn't believe my eyes.

Not my problem, I thought. *Head down.* In less than two years I'd be gone.

So I tried to keep out of everyone's way, but there's always a nice kid, isn't there? One who wants to integrate the newbie into the gang. *Come and sit with us! Come to the party!* I tried my hardest to avoid them, ate my lunch as far away from everyone else as I could, round the back of the art block, looking out over the field. It was pretty peaceful. Until that day.

I realized that … well, in my efforts to keep out of everyone's way I'd walked straight into the same shit I was trying to get away from. If I could rewind and go to, like, the canteen instead, then, believe me, I would. But I saw what I saw, and even though – after what happened at my last school – I wasn't going to say anything to anyone else, I figured, due diligence.

So I went to that girl's party for one reason and one reason only. To warn Ylsa.

Girls like her think they have power, that they can wrap people round their fingers, but it's just an illusion. When someone with real power decides they want something from them, they'll just take it.

And everyone wants to own beauty. It's evolutionary. Human beings love symmetrical faces. We give those people better jobs, better pay, we trust them more – pretty privilege, face card, all that shit. And even with nice guys – intelligent, thoughtful guys – when that burning ray of physical beauty is turned on them, they just can't resist.

And he *wasn't* a nice guy, whatever he tried to project. He was a manipulative sociopath.

But Ylsa didn't want to hear it. I guess when you get used to feeling powerful, you don't really … I don't know … clock it, when suddenly you're not in control any more. That's what manipulators do so well. You never know how vulnerable you are until it's too late. When I tried to tell her, she actually threatened me with her big bad dad. Because the truth doesn't just hurt, the truth makes people angry. And when there's a chance that the truth is going to threaten something we care about, the truth can make us kill.

The Exam

9:30–9:45

Zaina can't breathe, can't swallow, can only stare up at the handsome teacher's profile, waiting for it to turn in her direction. Mr Peters must have seen Nero speaking into the phone, and the logical conclusion to draw is that he was giving answers to someone still in the exam hall. This is it. She's out, and in the worst possible way: reported for cheating. Surely she'll have to tell the unis she's applying to. Will it have to appear on her CV for ever? For the first time since he died, she is glad her dad isn't here. At least he doesn't have to witness her public shaming.

And now Mr Peters is turning his head in her direction, making the connection between her and Nero, the best friends (as far as he knows), one of whom would do just about anything to get the grades she needs, including asking her friend to give her the answers. Her eyes are locked on the teacher's face, on his clear blue eyes, waiting for them to fall on her, on the dome of white plastic glinting in her ear.

But they don't.

They slide straight past her to the assembly-room door, through which Miss Zita is hurrying, her heels clacking on the parquet. Taking advantage of this wonderful deus ex machina, Zaina snatches the AirPod from her ear and stuffs it into her pocket.

The head of maths looks flustered. Her blonde hair – usually sleek – is ruffled, and there's a line of peach at her jaw where she hasn't worked her foundation in properly. She's around Zaina's mum's age but looks ten years younger. She's slimmer; her clothes are more expensive and better cut; she never has grey roots; her teeth are whiter. Some of the boys even fancy her, but only the ones who don't have lessons with her, because she's also a complete and utter cow. She has her favourites, mostly the prettier girls. In class, she always picks on the people who don't have their hands up and then, as they struggle to answer, she will sigh and roll her eyes. If they get the answer wrong, she'll shake her head and exchange smug smiles with a favoured student (often Ylsa). Once she reduced an eighteen-year-old boy to tears, after which she donned a look of fake sympathy and asked if he was sure maths was "the right subject" for him. This was two-thirds into the course and too late for him to change. Her nickname is Zitface, of course.

Miss Zita self-consciously tucks her white shirt into her fuchsia-pink skirt as Mr Peters pads over to her. Their conversation is whispered but with Nero gone there are no students between her and the door and Zaina can just make out what they're saying.

"Jon, I am so sorry. I just couldn't find my damned pass. I had it yesterday. I wouldn't mind, but if you don't check into the car park with it, they ticket you."

"No problem. I'm glad you made it OK."

Miss Zita glances furtively around the room and lowers her voice. "I'm actually a bit concerned a student took it."

"Why would they do that?"

"To have a look at the paper, I suppose. They could have used it to get into M1."

"It probably just fell off your bag. That's why I always

wear mine round my neck." He pats the pass against his chest, with its black-and-white shot that makes him look like a movie star.

"Noted, Jon." She gives him a tight smile. "And you're probably right. It's just that one of them came to me after class yesterday and started grilling me about parametric equations, and it's not like Nero Adams to be interested."

"Nero?" Mr Peters says.

"It was right after that conversation I noticed my pass was missing."

Zaina's heart clutches. She glances back at the science-block roof. Nero is gone. Craning her neck, she sees that he has scrambled down on to the porch and is now lowering his legs over the edge, to drop to the path that runs between the two buildings. Landing lightly, he straightens up and looks up at her.

"Can you manage here for a while?" Mr Peters is saying. "I just want to go and check on something."

Zaina's head whips round in time to see Mr Peters crossing to the door and striding out of the exam room while Miss Zita walks briskly to the invigilator's desk, patting her hair.

Back in the day Zaina and Nero could finish one

another's sentences; they always knew what each other was thinking and a sidelong glance would be enough to reduce them both to fits of giggles. She just has to hope he understands her now as she looks back at him and widens her eyes in warning. *Go! Now!* He nods, turns on his heel and ducks through the door of the science block.

Zaina exhales so loudly Miss Zita looks sharply at her. Ducking, Zaina picks up her pen, and pretends to be thinking. She can feel the teacher's gaze, but when she risks another glance though her hair, she sees that the teacher's attention has moved on.

The clock reads 9:37.

There's nothing she can do to help Nero now. With luck, he's had the sense to leave the school premises entirely. He's thrown his final paper away, but if Mr Peters doesn't manage to catch up with him, he's in the clear; they can't prove he stole Miss Zita's pass or that he was cheating. But if she knows Nero, once he's got an idea in his mind he won't be able to shake it. He's probably still planning to look for Chanelle.

Not my problem.

Her breathing is finally slowing back down to normal. She needs to get on.

She makes some schoolgirl errors in the next question, errors she almost doesn't notice and that would have taken at least three marks off her score. As a consequence, it doesn't take long for her anxiety for Nero to morph back into irritation and then suspicion. The forty-five minutes that are left of the exam might not even be enough time to finish the paper, let alone check her work. If Nero wanted to screw her over, he's achieved his aim perfectly. If he was just trying to distract her, she could have ignored him or had him thrown out, but the story he constructed about Chanelle reeled her in a treat. It almost had her convinced. Did he just spot Chanelle's empty desk and spin the tale because he knew she'd be drawn in?

He always did have an imagination. During nights at the hospital when she couldn't sleep, he would tell her bedtime stories down the phone, tales he made up on the spot, with stalwart heroines struggling against demon kings and necromancer curses to fulfil their epic quests. Usually she would drift off halfway through and miss the ending, but he would still be on the line when she woke up again.

Is he using this storytelling talent against her? Is this just a cynical attempt to try to stop her achieving her academic dream as revenge for her rejection of him?

But he'd sounded so earnest, she would bet her life that he actually believed what he was telling her.

Does the story even make sense?

Her brow creases as she goes over what he told her. Last night Nero saw Chanelle trying to get into M1 and then possibly being confronted by someone who was already inside. This morning she didn't turn up for the exam. Maybe the two events are connected, but that doesn't mean Chanelle's lying in a bloody heap somewhere. It would make more sense that she didn't turn up because whoever caught her trying to get into M1 was a teacher and they told her not to bother coming in for the exam. If the college knows she cheated on this paper, they might cancel her other two maths papers. Or all of them. Maybe she'll have to retake the entire year at a different college. Yes, she's probably upset and disappointed, but that doesn't mean she's in mortal danger: Nero has put two and two together and made five. He always was better at English than maths.

She needs to put all this out of her mind and concentrate on the paper.

Finding her place on the page, she reads the next question. This one is about curve equations, which she's normally pretty good at, and soon enough she is fully focused again. It doesn't matter that the room is getting hotter and more airless, that the scratching sound has started up again, that unlike Mr Peters with his considerate choice of soft-soled shoes, Miss Zita has chosen to wear high heels that clack loudly up and down each aisle as she stalks between the desks, because Zaina is back in flow, where she should be, the numbers and symbols pouring out of her as easy as breathing. She writes a congruent sign, a parenthesis, a square root symbol, a seven, a six.

76.

The pen stutters to a halt.

Chanelle's locker.

Nero's right about one thing. Chanelle must have been in this morning because her bag is in the locker room. But that doesn't mean she never went home last night. Maybe she just got a slap on the wrist for trying to get into M1 and was allowed to sit the exam as usual. Although this means she came into school but never made it to the exam room...

Why?

The scratching continues, just on the edge of her hearing. Saff has started to shake again.

Why?

Saff's broad back expands as they breathe, spilling out over the sides of the chair. Their arms never quite hang by their sides because of the bulging lats. They can bench press two-fifty. At the party Saff was angry at Chanelle, really angry. Angry enough to lash out.

Zaina can remember the look on Chanelle's face when she realized she was bleeding. She was scared. And Zaina wouldn't have blamed her. Walking past the pitches one day, Zaina was unlucky enough to be on the receiving end of a football in the back – kicked by Saff – that actually left a bruise. That was just a friendly kickabout. What is Saff capable of when they're not feeling so friendly?

Zaina hasn't been up on the gossip of the year group for a long time but, thinking back to the last maths exam, she can remember Chanelle standing on her own, where normally she and Saff would be joined at the hip. Was the row at the party serious enough for them to split up?

The reason Saff and Chanelle had got together, so the story went, was when Chanelle was being bothered by some guys on her way home on the bus. Saff had punched the emergency exit button and physically thrown them out on the street when the bus was still moving. It was a pretty cool thing to do, but also impulsive and aggressive. All the times Zaina and Chanelle had been sniping at one another, she'd always had in the back of her mind that she wouldn't want to be on the receiving end of an angry Saff.

Break-ups could be messy and drawn-out. What if Saff had tried to speak to Chanelle today, before the exam? What if it hadn't gone well? If Saff tried to stop Chanelle leaving, as Nero had to Zaina in the toilets, it might have got physical. If Saff pushed Chanelle, like at the party, she might have been really hurt. Hurt so badly she couldn't even sit the exam?

Is that why Saff's shaking? Because this time it's worse than a split lip?

Could Nero be right? Could Chanelle be in serious danger?

She glances out of the window, but there's no sign of him. And then, as she turns her back to the front of the room, Saff's hand slowly rises.

Miss Zita is watching the ranks of students like a hawk

166

and it takes a split second for her to notice. Her expression sours and she clip-clops over to Saff.

Miss Zita always misgenders Saff, and though she has been spoken to about it on more than one occasion, she always claims it's an honest mistake. Now as she approaches Saff her nostrils flare as if they have detected an unpleasant odour.

"What is it?" she says with little attempt to lower her voice.

Saff murmurs something.

"I beg your pardon?" Miss Zita says, then her expression turns to a grimace as Saff gets up from the desk. Rising to their full six feet, they tower over the petite teacher and this time their explanation is apparently acceptable to Miss Zita, who nods curtly. When Saff sets off across the room, Miss Zita backs away so fast she comes up against Poppy's chair and almost falls into her lap.

Poppy turns and glances at Zaina, suppressing a smile.

The door opens and Saff walks out into the corridor but, instead of taking a right to the toilet, they go left and the cropped blue head vanishes out of sight. Miss Zita is already walking back to the front of the room and clearly didn't notice that Saff went the wrong way. Maybe Zaina is the only one who did. Where are they going? To sort out whatever it is that's been causing them such stress for the past hour?

Poppy is still looking at Zaina, questioningly. They have known each other long enough to know when something is wrong. *What?* Poppy mouths.

Ylsa's desk is beside Poppy's and, noticing the exchange, she too turns round to look at Zaina. Her pretty face is blotchy and swollen from crying.

Ignoring them both, Zaina raises her hand.

Miss Zita's heels clack back across the parquet and she thrusts her head at Zaina. "What is it?"

"Can I go to the toilet please?"

"Saffron has just gone and I can't risk you running into each other. You'll have to wait."

"My period's started and it's going to come through my trousers if I wait."

They eye one another. One more warning from a pastoral point of view and Miss Zita might very well find herself out of a job. She probably knows that Zaina knows that. But she's just had her authority challenged by Saff in front of the whole class, and maybe her pride will come before good sense.

Zaina can sense several pairs of eyes on her now: Tabitha, Ylsa and Poppy have all turned in their chairs to look at her.

She must go now or she'll never catch up with Saff. Reaching between her legs she grimaces, then withdraws her hand.

"Look, Miss, it's coming through already."

The bluff works. Miss Zita averts her gaze with an expression of distaste. "Go, then, but don't be long."

The corridor outside the exam room is deserted. The only route away from the hall that Zaina can be sure Saff didn't take is the one that leads right, to the toilet. By turning left, they could either have gone to the classrooms on that side of the building, or taken the stairs down to reception and gone outside. That would have given them access to the whole school.

She sets off at a run towards the red door and bursts into the stairwell. Through the large window she can see that the path leading to and from the building is deserted. Either Saff has moved very fast or they're still in the building.

Then, some distance away, down the corridor to her left, she hears the characteristic whump of one of the internal doors. Crossing the stairwell, she hurries in the direction of the sound.

The doors lining this corridor are windowless and, without the overhead strip lights, sunk in an oppressive gloom.

In her rush to catch up with Saff, who now has several minutes head start, she bangs through the first set of internal doors and one of them strikes the wall with a rifle crack. She pauses, wincing, and as the echoes die away she hears the squeak of trainers up ahead where the corridor bisects. She runs on, light-footed, and, reaching the junction, catches a flash of Saff's hulking figure disappearing into a room halfway up the corridor.

It's one of the language rooms. As far as Zaina remembers, in addition to maths Saff does sports science and biology.

Moving quickly and silently up the gloomy hallway she pauses outside the door and listens.

All is quiet.

What could Saff possibly be doing in there?

Maybe nothing. Maybe Saff just needed some air, or maybe they have hidden some kind of exam materials to consult. But why store them here, so far from the exam room? So far out of sight or hearing?

Too far for Mr Peters, Miss Zita or Mrs Hatcher to hear a scream. Could Chanelle be in there? In need of help? Alone, she wouldn't have a chance against Saff.

Where the hell is Nero? If Zaina made the connection, then surely he could have worked it out?

Scanning the corridor, she sees a fire extinguisher hanging on the wall. Creeping over, she lifts it from its hooks. It's much heavier than she expects and she almost drops it; the clang would certainly alert Saff to her presence. A blast of foam probably wouldn't hold them back for long, but at least it might give Zaina a few moments' head start.

She creeps over and opens the door a crack. Empty desks stretch away to the back of the room. There is no sign of Chanelle.

Then Zaina remembers the language rooms connect with internal doors. Perhaps Saff has gone through to the one next door. Gingerly she pushes the door open and tiptoes into the room, pausing by the teacher's desk and listening intently. All she can hear is the blood pulsing in her ears.

"Why are you following me?"

She jumps violently and spins round.

Saff's huge figure is standing between her and the exit.

"Get away from me!" Zaina cries, backing up, but she only gets a few steps before she comes up sharply against the teacher's desk. Saff's ice-grey eyes are thunderous as they take a step forward. And then another. Zaina presses the button on the fire extinguisher. Nothing happens. The yellow safety clip is still attached. She fumbles at the nozzle, trying to pull it off.

"What the hell are you doing?"

She glances up and does a double take. Saff's meaty arms are folded across their chest, not outstretched to throttle her.

"What am *I* doing?" Zaina splutters. "What are *you* doing?"

"I'd say that's my business."

"We're supposed to be in an exam!"

"Exactly. So why the hell are you following me?"

Giving up on the spray nozzle, Zaina clamps the extinguisher under her arm, trying not to show any sign of strain. The heaviest weight she's lifted recently is her pen with a full cartridge of ink, but Saff doesn't need to know she's barely able to hold the fire extinguisher let alone use it as a weapon.

"Where's Chanelle?"

Saff frowns. "What?"

"You heard."

"I … I don't know."

Zaina searches Saff's face for any flicker of guilt but their expression is unreadable. "You left the exam to go to the toilet and then you came down here. Why?"

"I didn't leave to go to the toilet, not that it's any of your bloody business."

"Chanelle's not in the exam."

Saff looks confused at the apparent non sequitur. "Yeah, I noticed."

"Why?"

"I don't know. I haven't spoken to her for a while."

If Saff's lying, they're one hell of an actor. "You didn't speak to her this morning before the exam?"

"I told you, we haven't spoken in ages. Not since the party, actually. Why are you asking me? What's this about?"

"I'm worried about her."

Saff gives a derisive snort. "Because she's not in the exam? I'd have thought you and Ylsa would be rubbing your hands."

"Why do you think she isn't there?"

Saff's shoulders drop. "I don't know. I figured she just couldn't face it. Because of what happened with us maybe, or because the exam stress got too much for her. There has to be a better way than this to measure people's worth, don't you think? With people like Chan – clever, sensitive, hard-working people – it doesn't show what they're capable of, it just breaks them."

Zaina exhales a little. Saff's distress seems authentic. "Do you think she could be self-harming?"

Saff shakes her head. "When we got together, I asked her what I could do to help with that and we worked on things. She got better. Even in the run-up to the exams she just used meditation and stuff to keep in control."

Fairly certain she isn't in immediate danger, Zaina lowers the extinguisher to the floor. "Do you think she was stressed enough to try to cheat?"

Saff frowns. "What?"

"Someone saw her trying to get into the room where the papers were being stored."

Saff sighs wearily. "I don't know. She was under a lot of pressure."

"From her parents?"

"Yeah, of course. Aren't we all? Every day I have to live

174

with the fact that mine think I murdered their daughter. But not just her parents, right?" Saff looks pointedly at her.

Zaina blinks. "What, me?"

"And Ylsa. Always trying to get one over on each other. If Chan did decide to cheat, it would be to try to keep up with the two of you. At her secondary school she won all the prizes for maths and science, and then she comes here and has to share them out with you two. It hurt her pride."

"And I'm supposed to apologize for that?"

"Don't be a dick, Zaina. I didn't mean that. I think the whole thing is crap: the way we compare ourselves to each other all the time. Who's the prettiest, the most ripped, the coolest, the most popular. It just makes you feel bad about yourself. I don't give a shit about any of it. As long as I had Chan and my sport I was happy." They look away, frowning hard. Was the mighty Saff Jackson about to cry? But after a brief struggle to regain their composure, Saff turns on her angrily. "So, you followed me because you think I had something to do with Chanelle missing the exam?"

"I saw you fight at the party," Zaina says. "I saw what happened." The extinguisher is a red blur by her feet. If Saff went for her, would she have time to snatch it up?

But Saff's anger drains away as quickly as it appeared. "I

never meant to hurt her. I was upset, but it wasn't Chan's fault ... and I shouldn't have taken it out on her."

It's then that Zaina notices something that makes her heart contract.

Saff's left hand is balled into a fist at their side, as if they are trying to hide something, something that has stained their palm red.

Saff follows her gaze, then their eyes lock.

"Why is your hand bleeding?" Zaina says softly.

"It's not."

"Show me."

She starts to back away as Saff raises their arm, turns it and opens it to reveal a handful of pills.

Zaina's eyes widen. "You're not..."

Saff gives a snort. "Taking an overdose? They're Skittles. My hand's hot so the colour's bled out."

"Skittles?"

Saff's mouth drops open. "Jesus, what, you thought I'd *murdered* Chanelle?"

"Well, you've got to admit you've been behaving weirdly."

"OK, fine, Zaina. I didn't want this getting out, but if you really have to know." Saff sighs and sinks down on the corner of the teacher's desk, making it creak. "After the mocks I'd been feeling a bit shit, but I didn't know what it was and then one morning my mum couldn't wake me up. I was rushed into A & E and diagnosed with type one diabetes." They pause, running a hand through sweat-damp hair. Always pale, Saff's face has taken on a grey tinge. "After the doctors told me what I'd have to do from now on to keep my blood sugar in check, I knew I'd have to quit the football team. I'd be a liability. I was OK about it, until I got to the party and all the guys were there and everyone was going on about me quitting and trying to get me to come back. I didn't want to admit why – it felt like weakness, you know? – and I guess I just saw red. Chanelle said I should just tell them and go back to playing, that there were loads of diabetics in professional sport, but I get mood swings when my bloods aren't right and I'd been drinking. I thought she just didn't get it." Saff looks up, their eyes pleading. "I swear I didn't mean to hurt her."

It's then that Zaina notices Saff is still trembling, more violently than before, and as she watches, the sturdy football star begins to list sideways.

Springing forward, Zaina catches Saff and guides the hand with the sweets in to their mouth. Afterwards, she holds Saff upright and the weight of the warm body against her chest, the cropped hair brushing her chin, and the musk of fresh sweat stirs something inside her solar plexus. Something physical that connects her heart and her brain to her nerve endings and is not trivial at all. She's almost sorry when Saff's trembling finally subsides and they straighten up, blinking and rubbing their forehead.

"Thanks. I'm still figuring this out."

Zaina's about to tell Saff that it can't simply be that Chanelle is too scared to come into school because her bag is the locker, so she must be here somewhere, but before she can speak quick footsteps approach down the corridor.

"Saff, is that you?"

Saff glances at the door. "It's Miss Iggle. Go, or we'll be disqualified."

By the time the school nurse opens the door, Zaina has slipped into the adjoining room.

"I thought I heard voices." Miss Iggle is a funny little owl-eyed woman with a severe grey crop and rather strange taste in clothes. Peering through the crack in the door, Zaina sees that on this excessively hot day she is wearing an Aran jumper over a tartan skirt and Hunter wellies.

"I was having a hypo, Miss. I might have been talking to myself, sorry."

The teacher bustles over and frowns up into Saff's face. "Oh dear, oh dear, you must be more careful. You know your blood sugar gets low with stress and excessive heat. You should have come straight to me."

"I was on my way and I started feeling ill. Sorry, Miss. I just had some sweets, so I think I'll be all right now."

"Well, come to my room and we'll test to make sure. We don't want it going too high. I'll let Miss Zita know that I'll supervise your extra time at the end."

"I really think I'll be OK," Saff protests, but they are no match for the diminutive Miss Iggle, who propels them out of the door and down the corridor to her office.

As the echoes of their footsteps die away, Zaina goes back into the empty room. Dust motes spin in the eddies from their departure. She stares at the blank whiteboard, as if the answer to this strange mystery will somehow appear there.

So Chanelle hasn't been self-harming recently. This should make her feel a lot better. But it doesn't; it makes her feel worse. Because if Chanelle is not locked in a toilet cutting herself, then where is she?

Trudging back down the corridor, she reaches the stairwell, where the long window looks out across the staff car park. Mrs Hatcher is waddling across to her little hatchback, talking on the phone. She must have decided that no one was likely to come in this late for the exam and is heading for home.

Zaina freezes. Mrs Hatcher's words to Mr Peters this morning have just come back to her. A parent had rung in looking for their missing daughter. *I will certainly let you know if she turns up, yes. Like I say, she was definitely in school yesterday.*

Is the missing girl Chanelle?

MRS GLORIA HATCHER

RECORDED INTERVIEW

Date: 28th June
Location: South Harrow Police Station
Time: 10:23
Conducted by officers from the Met Police

POLICE: Thanks for coming in, Mrs Hatcher.

GH: I considered it my duty, officer. After yesterday's terrible, terrible events. I mean, it was so unbelievable. Goodness me. In my own school. My phone's been ringing off the hook for the past day. *Gloria, what on earth has happened? Are you OK?* But I said, *I'm sorry, but I cannot talk to you about it until I've told the police what I know.*

POLICE: Thank you. We would ask people not to speculate until—

GH: I took the call, in the morning. Did you know that? From Mrs Goldstein. She was in an awful state. As you would be. She'd been up all night waiting for Chanelle to get in touch. She hadn't called you in at that point, because Chanelle does go off sometimes, particularly when she is stressed. Usually to be with her partner Saff. Did you know they were together?

POLICE: We—

GH: School receptionists know this sort of thing. Young people confide in us. I'm not their parents or their teachers. I'm not going to tell them off, or judge them like their peers. I'm just a warm ear. I listen, like a favourite auntie.

POLICE: Did one of the injured students confide in you?

GH: Well, I mean, I'm friendly with all the students. I can't say I remember any specific… Anyway, the point is, you hear things in my position. You know what's *really* going on, far more than the head even. She comes to me to find out what's going on in her own school!

POLICE: So what did you actually know?

GH: I can tell you my theory. My hunch if you like. Sometimes I think I should have been a detective myself, honestly. I love true crime, don't you? Well, of course you do, ha ha!

POLICE: Your theory, Mrs Hatcher?

GH: A love triangle. Nero Adams, Zaina Abbour and Chanelle Goldstein. What happened was a crime of passion. You know in France they use that as a defence?

POLICE: What evidence do you have for this?

GH: I don't have "evidence", officer. That's your job! I am

giving you the benefit of my knowledge and experience of young people. It's up to you to prove it.

POLICE: So this love triangle…

GH: Nero Adams. Such a shame. What a lovely boy: charming, good-looking. Always used to call me "Mrs H". *How was your weekend, Mrs H?* If I were twenty years younger… Well, they were thick as thieves, Nero and Zaina. Always together. And then suddenly they weren't. No more shared lunches, no walking to class together. I wondered what it was at the time, but now I understand. There'd always been beef between Zaina and Chanelle. Oh sorry, "beef" is a word the young people use for bad feeling. It must have been because she suspected Nero liked Chanelle. And then, around the time of the exam, something happened. My guess is that Zaina discovered them together, *in flagrante*, as it were. Well, you know what girls are like. Hell hath no fury, et cetera.

POLICE: You think Zaina Abbour tried to kill Chanelle Goldstein and Nero Adams because of jealousy?

GH: The most powerful human emotion, officer.

POLICE: One of them. There are others.

The Exam

9:45–10:00

Mrs Hatcher's hatchback putters out of the car park. The gossipy receptionist is usually cheerful and chatty, but on the way to her car she'd looked worried. No wonder, if a parent is calling the school first thing in the morning because their child didn't come home the previous night.

Zaina's brow creases in thought. If the child was Chanelle, then she vanished right after seeing whatever she saw in Room M1. And yet she still took the time to stash her bag back in her locker.

That's strange.

But what is Zaina supposed to do with this information?

Tell a teacher? Get her phone from the locker room and call the police?

Or is she barking up the wrong tree completely, in which case she'll be throwing away her A-level for the sake of her rival who is perfectly OK?

Without knowing what else to do, she heads back to the exam hall and retakes her seat.

Miss Zita is walking past Chanelle's empty desk on her way back to the front of the room. After the call to Mrs Hatcher, the school is obviously aware she's missing. The only thing they might not know is that her bag is in the locker. But if Zaina mentions this, and Miss Zita takes it seriously, what can she realistically do? Chanelle is eighteen and Zaina knows from TV crime shows that when someone reaches eighteen the police don't look for them with the same urgency as they do children.

It's possible that Chanelle might simply have abandoned her bag and walked out of school. Back when her dad was getting sicker, Zaina was always on edge for some new and horrible emergency. Sometimes she felt like running away. Maybe after the stress of her break-up with Saff and the exam pressure, Chanelle felt the same. Maybe she's not on the school premises at all, but wandering through the park or sitting in a cafe somewhere for some peace. If she was still here, surely Nero would have found her by now. Maybe he's been trying to tell Zaina just that.

While Miss Zita is still facing in the other direction, she delves into her pocket, retrieves the AirPod and slips it into her ear, pulling her hair down to cover it.

It is completely silent.

She cranes her neck to peer out of the window but there's no sign of him on the science-block roof or the path below. Perhaps Mr Peters discovered him and ejected him from the premises, though if this was the case, the teacher would probably have come back to the exam hall. Or perhaps Nero did find Chanelle and summoned Mr Peters. In which case it's out of Zaina's hands now and she should just get on with what's left of the paper.

She is reaching to her ear to remove the AirPod when a figure blocks out the light. Zaina looks up into Miss Zita's scowl.

The blood drains from her face and her hand drops to her side. She's been caught. And Miss Zita is no friendly, flirty Mr Peters. She's harsh at the best of times – last year the student who she reported had written a single formula on his wrist – but getting information through an AirPod is probably the worst and most damning sort of cheating possible. There's a good chance all her exam papers will be called into question. A very likely chance that she'll be expelled and have to retake the year at a different sixth form, where everyone will know her as *the cheat*.

Miss Zita looks down the right-angle triangle of her nose at Zaina. Zaina opens her mouth to try to explain that she wasn't receiving the answers, but that she and Nero were worried about their missing classmate and were exchanging information about where she could be. It sounds so contrived. And besides, her voice won't come.

"I have been informed," Miss Zita says coldly, "that your toilet trip was the second such trip you took in the past hour. Are you seriously expecting me to believe you suddenly came on in such a brief amount of time, and so heavily that it was coming through your underwear?"

Zaina stares at her. What can she say to get herself out of this? A bead of sweat trickles from her hairline down her left temple.

Miss Zita folds her arms and her eyes narrow with

malice. "I'd like an explanation, or you will be leaving this exam right now."

Zaina swallows hard and opens her mouth.

There is a sudden loud crash. Miss Zita's head whips round.

Poppy has collapsed. Some of the students are already out of their seats and on their way over to help, but Miss Zita barks at them to *sit down!* as she hurries across to the girl lying face down and motionless on the floor.

Crouching beside her she shakes her shoulder. "Poppy? Talk to me please. Poppy?"

Zaina stares, her heart in her mouth. What is wrong with her friend? If it's something serious she will never forgive herself. But Poppy starts to stir, raising her hand to her head and rubbing a spot on her forehead.

"That's it," Miss Zita says, and with surprising tenderness begins to help Poppy back into her chair. Kneeling beside her, the teacher hands her the bottle of water and watches anxiously as she drinks.

"All right?" she murmurs when Poppy puts the bottle down. "Do you think you're strong enough to make it to Miss Iggle's office on your own? I can't leave the exam and I don't know where Mr Peters is."

"It's fine," Poppy murmurs, still rubbing her head. "I don't need to see Miss Iggle. It's just so hot in here. I felt a bit faint, but I'm OK now."

"You collapsed, Poppy. That's not *feeling a bit faint*. I'm going to ask for a volunteer to take you."

"No, please, Miss. I'm OK. I want to finish the exam."

Miss Zita reaches forward and pulls Poppy's hand away from her head, frowning unhappily at the red lump forming at her hairline. "You might have really hurt yourself. I can't just let you sit here with a head injury."

"It's only half an hour to the end of the exam, and then I promise I'll go to Miss Iggle. It was nothing, really, just a little bump."

Miss Zita bites her lip.

"The paper's going really well, and I need that A, Miss."

Clever Poppy to know that Miss Zita values academic achievement way above physical safety.

The teacher sighs unhappily. "It is hot in here. I'll prop the door open, and that should give us a through draft, but you *must* tell me if you start to feel unwell again."

Poppy promises.

After grabbing her chin and looking carefully into

each of her eyes, Miss Zita stands and hurries across the room to the door. It takes her several attempts to prop the heavy door open, and she eventually manages to do so by using paper folded into a tight wedge. Even then the airflow is negligible, but she can do no more. Returning to Poppy's desk, she checks again that Poppy is OK (almost like a person with normal levels of compassion and empathy), then makes her way back to the front of the room. There she turns and narrows her eyes, as if she's playing Grandma's Footsteps and is determined to catch any student daring to creep up on her.

"Excitement over. Get back to your work. You have forty-five minutes left, and I know for a fact that most of you will need every one of those minutes." And then her eyes flick to Zaina's. Zaina winces, waiting for the axe to fall. "That includes you, Miss Abbour."

Zaina blinks. Did Miss Zita just let her off? The teacher is famous for sweating the small stuff – reporting you for wearing non-reg socks or having your top shirt button undone – but could it be that Poppy's collapse put the extra toilet trip into perspective? Whatever the reason, Zaina offers up a silent prayer of thanks, then does as she's told and goes back to her paper.

Becoming aware, a minute later, that there are still eyes on her, she peers through her hair to check that Miss Zita isn't still glaring at her and finds that the gaze belongs to Poppy. Looking over her shoulder at Zaina, Poppy smiles and winks.

Zaina stares in astonishment. Was the fainting fit just an act to rescue her from the ire of Miss Zita? Her heart swells with gratitude. In the deepest part of herself, she always wanted to forgive Poppy, and now, finally, Poppy has given her a reason to. She blinks at her best friend, her lips quivering into something like a smile. The feeling is like blood flowing again through a vein that had been blocked up. Poppy's eyes shine in the light lancing through the windows and, as they hold one another's gaze, the distance between them falls away.

A tear trickles down Poppy's cheek and then she nods meaningfully at Zaina's paper, then turns to get on with hers.

It's then that Zaina notices another head has twisted to look at her, but this one's expression is far less friendly.

Ylsa looks awful. Her mascara has drawn black streaks down her cheeks, and her lipstick is smeared across her jaw. But her expression is no longer of distress but sneering smugness. Zaina realizes with a jolt that it must have been Ylsa who complained to Miss Zita about her going to the toilet twice, probably hoping to get her kicked out of the exam, and now she's pissed off that Poppy rescued her. What kind of a dick would do something like that, especially considering what she's been up to herself?

Ylsa turns round but Zaina stares at her back, breathing more heavily. She never realized Ylsa hated her so much. Then she becomes aware of the pressure of the AirPod in her left ear. With her eyes fixed on Miss Zita's blonde head, she reaches up and takes it out. In all that time it hasn't made a single noise and now she sees why. The tiny white light on the pod is flashing, which means it is no longer paired with Nero's phone.

Is that because he's out of range? Did he turn off his Bluetooth because he's found Chanelle – or been found by Mr Peters? Either way there must have been a way to let her know, even if it was just to reconnect his phone with the AirPod and allow her to overhear the conversation.

She never did hear the ends of Nero's stories.

The clock reads 9:56.

The pen feels strange in her hand when she picks it up.

The dents in her fingers throb as the pen presses into them. The inscription glares up at her.

OK. No more distractions. I've got this. I won't let you down, Daddy.

Question sixteen.

It begins with the words *Explain why*, and then there is a long and complicated equation. This is followed by *May be approximated by*, then there are more numbers, letters, brackets, symbols and arrows, before the final part of the question: *for suitable values for* a *and* b.

She's been out of the zone for so long she can't focus straight away. She reads the question again, then a movement outside catches her attention and her gaze snaps to the science-block roof. It's just the seagull strutting along the tarmac. Feeling her gaze, it turns its sharp head and fixes her with eyes like beads of black ink.

She reads the question a third time but when she gets to the end the beginning has flown out of her mind.

Her eyes return to the science block, searching the bank of windows for any movement, but it's dark inside the block and they only reflect the building opposite, the one Zaina is sitting in. If there were more stories to the block, she would see her own face looking back at her.

Explain why…
May be approximated by…
For suitable values for…

She throws the pen down and presses the heels of her hands into her eye sockets.

Something is wrong; she's just not sure what it is.

Opening her eyes she takes a deep breath. OK. She's a mathematician. She just needs to use the same method she would use to tackle any difficult problem: break it down into its parts and figure them out systematically. She has all the necessary information after all:

Chanelle saw something in Room M1.

The school received a panicked phone call from the parent of a missing child.

Mrs Hatcher's responses to the parent implied that Chanelle hadn't been home since school yesterday.

Chanelle's bag is in her locker.

There were spots of blood on Zaina and Nero's paper.

Explain why…

But she can't.

Unless… She frowns. Could the solution to the mystery be what she thought right at the beginning? *Your first answer is usually the right one*, the maths YouTubers tell you. *Don't overthink things.*

Saff seemed so sure that Chanelle wasn't self-harming, but you hide things from the people that are closest to you. When Dad was finally diagnosed, he admitted that he'd been having symptoms for months. He hadn't said anything because he didn't want to worry them.

Saff might have been right: Chanelle *did* stop cutting herself, but she and Saff broke up at the time of the greatest exam pressure Chanelle had ever experienced. If she was going to start self-harming again, wouldn't it be now? Especially if she was caught by a teacher trying to cheat. The teacher most likely to have been in M1 was Miss Zita. Zitface wouldn't even have given Chanelle a chance to explain, she'd have taken sadistic pleasure in telling Chanelle just how screwed she really was. If anyone was going to make you take a knife to your own flesh, it was Franklyn Roberts Academy's head of maths.

Which means Zaina is right back to the answer she came up with at the beginning of the exam: Chanelle is somewhere in the school building. And she's probably not in a good way.

If Mr Peters has searched the school for Nero, there's

a good chance one of them will have found her and she might be getting the help she needs, but then why wouldn't Nero have let Zaina know?

She scans the area of the school she can see out of the window. For a few minutes she was distracted by Miss Zita and Poppy. Did she miss Mr Peters going into the science block? Did he find Nero? Is he giving him a talking-to right now? Surely Nero would have told the teacher why he was there, but maybe Mr Peters thought it was just an excuse.

In which case there's a chance Chanelle hasn't been found.

If she's even here on school premises. *If* she's actually in any trouble at all.

Is Zaina really sure the answer she's come up with is remotely plausible? *Go back, check your workings.* She's preparing herself to go over everything one more time when there is a blood-curdling shriek. It is caused by the legs of Ylsa's chair scraping across the floor as she pushes herself away from her desk, and now she gets up so fast the chair crashes to the floor.

All the heads in the exam room turn to look at her.

Ylsa's exam paper has slipped off the desk and is lying on the floor, and at first Zaina thinks she's got up to retrieve it. But she makes no move to do this, only stands there, breathing so heavily her shoulders heave. Miss Zita clip-clops over and mutters to her, peering anxiously into the face of her favourite pupil and touching Ylsa's arm.

Ylsa pulls away, then she spins on her heel and bolts for the open door. And then she is gone, her footsteps rattling away down the corridor, then thundering down the stairs.

There is a moment's stunned silence, then the faces turn back to their papers. Miss Zita watches the door helplessly, as if hoping Ylsa will reconsider and come back, then she bends and picks up Ylsa's chair. Retrieving the exam paper from the floor, she flicks through it, her face unreadable, then returns to the invigilator's desk.

Zaina looks out of the window, craning her neck to see down to the path. Ylsa does not appear. Where was she going in such a hurry?

And then her blood runs cold, because finally she realizes.

Ylsa stashed the answers to the paper in the toilet cistern, so she must have got them from M1 yesterday evening. Chanelle looked scared when the door opened because she had witnessed Ylsa cheating. Ylsa's father is a crook. She learned at her daddy's knee that to get what you wanted you had to be prepared to do anything.

What was the threat she spat at Tabitha at the party? *I will destroy you.* Rather than risk losing everything she had worked for, had Ylsa decided to destroy Chanelle too? In a more literal way. A way that left specks of blood on the uppermost pages of the stacks of question papers?

Ylsa is impetuous, fiery-tempered, bigger, stronger and meaner than Chanelle. Who knows what she is capable in the heat of the moment?

Is that what Ylsa's tears have been about today? Because she did something bad to Chanelle and now she can't live with it? If Zaina follows her now, will she lead her to Chanelle?

No, she tells herself firmly. This is madness. The cogs in her brain have overheated and are spinning out of control.

And yet something is definitely going on, because now there are four people loose in the school.

Chanelle.

Nero.

Mr Peters.

Ylsa.

It's like a horror film: a character goes missing so someone is sent to find them, and then *they* go missing, so someone else is sent after them, and so on… Zaina isn't going to be stupid enough to be the next person to vanish into the monster's jaws, is she?

Yes, it would appear she is.

Getting up from her seat she stands there, swaying slightly, her mouth opening and closing like a fish.

"Sit down, Miss Abbour," the teacher snarls at her.

The faces of her classmates turn again and Zaina catches first Poppy's eye, then Tabitha's. Poppy's are questioning but Tabitha's gaze is steady. Whatever Ylsa and Tabitha argued about at the party, there is a link to what's happening today; she's sure of it.

"Zaina Abbour. Sit down!"

"I've finished, Miss Zita."

"Then go back and check your paper."

"I have."

Their eyes lock. Zaina has never disobeyed a teacher in her life, not least the head of the subject she is hoping to study at university, who wrote her a glowing reference. The reference she could easily retract. Though that might be irrelevant now. Zaina is only three quarters of the way through the paper, and twenty-five per cent of the marks will mean the difference between an A and the A star she needs. They both know this.

"No, you cannot go," Miss Zita growls. "Sit down."

From the desk Zaina's pen glints, the gold inscription flashing in the sunlight, Morse-coding its disapproval.

"Sorry," she says to both of them. And then, without bothering to pick up her pencil case, water bottle or her father's last gift to her, she walks out of the exam.

Standing outside the assembly room, she experiences something close to a panic attack and has to steady herself on the wall, gasping for breath. What is she doing? Glancing back, she sees Miss Zita shaking her head as she gathers up her unfinished paper, her staccato elbow movements suggesting that opportunities for Zaina to change her mind are rapidly diminishing. What has she done?

Finally Miss Zita straightens up and walks away, the doorway framing Zaina's empty desk. The pen rolls slowly across the wood, flashing gold every time the inscription faces the sun, then drops to the floor with a soft clunk, disgorging a spatter of ink.

Zaina stares at the ink for some Rorschach message from beyond the grave. Are the dark spots her father's tears? The metaphorical blood he shed for her sake? As it runs between the strips of parquet, it forms the upper line of an exclamation mark.

Or it could simply be an "I".

I am doing this, Daddy, *for me*.

And, with that, she turns her back on the exam hall and walks away.

That's when the urgency of the situation strikes her. Ylsa is now several minutes ahead of her and could have got just about anywhere in the school by now.

Taking the stairs two at a time, Zaina bursts through the internal doors into the foyer. Standing by Mrs Hatcher's empty desk, she turns in a slow circle, wondering which direction the other girl took. It must have been either left, towards the humanities classrooms, right, towards the music rooms, or through the main doors and out of the building. This, surely, is the most likely option, as people have been pouring in and out all day, and if Ylsa had done something to Chanelle in this part of the building, there was a risk someone might have seen.

Is that seriously what Zaina thinks has happened?

But for the first time she has no clue how to answer this, and no idea of a method to find it other than the dunce's friend: trial and error.

She has pushed open the main doors when she hears a slam. It's too metallic and high-pitched to be either an internal or external door, and it's coming from beneath her feet.

The lockers!

Flying down the steps down to the basement, she sprints down the corridor and skids to a halt at the door of the locker room. She pauses a moment, trying to regulate her ragged breathing, then tiptoes up to the door. Pressing her face to the cool wood, she peers sidelong through the round window.

Ylsa is inside, rifling through her bag on the central bench. She's crying so hard she can't seem to see what she's doing and when she finally locates what she's looking for – her phone – she fumbles and drops it under the bench. Retrieving it, she jabs savagely at the screen before tucking it under her jaw as she zips the bag and slings it over her shoulder.

Who is she calling?

Before Zaina has time to find out, Ylsa is coming

straight at her. There is nowhere to go and Zaina can do nothing but press herself against the wall as Ylsa yanks open the door. Her heart jumps into her mouth. How will Ylsa react when she discovers she has been followed? Definitely not as calmly as Saff did. Will she act innocent or is she desperate enough to resort to violence?

But to her astonishment Ylsa does neither of these things. She simply ignores Zaina completely, sweeping past her as if she isn't even there, and goes stamping up the steps. She is halfway up when the call connects.

"I've fucking left, OK?"

There is a pause as the person on the other end speaks.

"Because *obviously* I couldn't fucking do it!"

Zaina goes up after her, the most obvious tail possible, but Ylsa is too distracted to notice. "No, Daddy, *you* listen. I don't *care* if I end up stacking shelves at Sainsbury's!" Reaching the top of the stairs, she jogs down the corridor, bangs through the internal doors and sweeps past Mrs Hatcher's empty desk, before bursting out into the sunshine.

Zaina goes after her in time to see a flock of birds explode from the plane tree behind the science block as Ylsa screeches, "NO I DO NOT WANT YOU TO COME AND PICK ME UP!"

Zaina watches her cross the car park and march through the college gates, her shrill voice echoing.

MISS YLSA MARCHANT

RECORDED INTERVIEW

Date: 29th June

Location: South Harrow Police Station

Time: 11:14

Conducted by officers from the Met Police

YM: My dad's super pissed off about this.

POLICE: We are well aware he did not want you talking to us, but we have come to believe that you are a key witness of the events that took place on the twenty-seventh of June.

YM: He said you threatened to look into his tax affairs. That was brave.

POLICE: As I said, we felt it was important that you talk to us.

YM: He also said you wanted to "eliminate me from your enquiries", which means you're under the mistaken impression I had something to do with this shitshow.

POLICE: We're not trying to catch you out or frame you, Ylsa, and, no, you are not a suspect, but you are an important witness. We need to get to the bottom of what happened to your friends.

YM: Are they OK?

POLICE: They're in the best possible hands.

YM (*whispered*): Fuck, fuck, fuck.

POLICE: If you're concerned about any repercussions

from your father after speaking to us, there are avenues we can go down.

YM: I'm not afraid of my dad, even if you are. He would never hurt me. Let's just get this over with.

POLICE: Just start at the beginning and take it slow.

YM: Well, I'm not going to start at the end, am I? Jesus. OK. OK, fine.

So, when I was little everyone used to call me a daddy's girl. *The way she looks at him, proper little daddy's girl.* My mum would snap back, "Well, all men love a bit of attention, don't they?", like she was jealous, and I was glad about that, even at, like, three. I knew I had more power over him than she did.

POLICE: So there were problems at home?

YM: That's not what I said. My dad worshipped me and everyone else just had to accept that or take it up with him. No one felt like doing that, because he can be, well ... you know. But not for me. For me he was a pussycat. I would make up little dance routines for him, sit on his knee when he came home from work, cry myself to sleep if he didn't get back in time to tuck me in. All my pictures were of Daddy – *Daddy and his trucks, Daddy in his big car, Daddy playing golf* – totally ignoring my mum. When he looked at me it was different to how he looked at other people. And the way *they* looked back at him – with fear – made me realize I was special. So I carried on.

POLICE: People were afraid of your father?

YM: They knew he'd do anything to get what he wanted.

POLICE: But you weren't?

YM: Like I said, he was different with me. My brothers were just "grunts" like him, he said. They were going to take over the family business – which isn't organized crime, whatever those dicks at Franklyn tell you. It's just construction. Yes, he's been inside, but he was really young and that was an accident. He didn't mean to knock the guy out.

So, anyway, my brothers were his mates, chips off the old block, *Dumb and Dumber*, but I was on this pedestal. I was pretty, of course (just like my mum was before she had all the *tweakments*, as she likes to call them). That definitely had something to do with it. Dads love their daughters to be beautiful, don't they? You got daughters, officer?

POLICE: I have, yes.

YM: Well, take my advice, don't bang on about them being beautiful.

My mum used to love buying me clothes and doing my hair. We would go to the beauty therapist together and have matching nails done. But my dad said none of that shit mattered. That the world was full of beautiful girls who'd just end up on the arm of some rich twat, who'd still beat her up on a Saturday night and leave her for a younger model when she hit forty. He didn't want me to be a princess. He wanted me to be a *queen*. Someone with real power, and he insisted the only way you got that was through education. Education he hadn't had access to, so he was gonna make sure I did.

My brothers went to the local state school, but I got sent to Lady Katherine, which was a private girls' school for all the footballers' kids. I was always top of the class because most of the other parents didn't care how their kids were doing, they just let the school handle it, but my dad was always checking my grades. I felt this massive pressure to do well, to justify his favouritism, but when I got to be a teenager and the work got harder, it was so much easier to just be pretty, you know? Concentrate on my Insta feed, getting my make-up and hair just right. The rewards were faster. It's the dopamine hit, isn't it? Every like gives you a little high. And I got loads of likes. Guys were always DMing me and even a famous footballer asked me for pictures. OnlyFans kind of stuff. I was fourteen and I didn't even tell my dad cos he would have ripped the guy's head off. Metaphorically – don't get excited.

Anyway, when the GCSEs came round, they got me a tutor, and at the last parents' evening before the end of Year Eleven my science teacher said I should consider medicine. My dad was beside himself. A doctor in the family was, like, his wet dream. (Though really a lawyer would have been more useful, right? Ha ha). My mum was totally gassed that I'd be able to give her Botox, which she already has way too much of by the way. She won't hear this, will she?

POLICE: I don't imagine your mother's Botox will be considered relevant to the case.

YM: Good. So, anyway, Dad decided I'd have more chance at medicine going to a state sixth form, so they took me out of Lady Katherine and sent me to Franklyn. It was a real shock, I can tell you. I don't know if you know anything about Franklyn, but it's a selective sixth form and you have to get all sevens and above at GCSE to have any chance of getting in. The kids that went there from the local state schools were crazy bright. They didn't need tutors and pushy parents to do well; they were just naturally clever. Like Nero Adams. If you want to know, then, yes, I liked him, and, yes, I suppose that made me even more determined to beat Zaina.

But Zaina wasn't so easy to beat. Nor was Chanelle. And suddenly I had to confess to my dad that I wasn't top of the class any more. The look on his face the first time

I admitted it. It was the first time in my life I'd seen disappointment when he'd looked at me. I cried all night. My eyes were so puffy the next day everyone noticed, and I had to make up some shit about my dog dying. You know Zaina's dad died, right? Well, she didn't get half the sympathy I got for my made-up dog, from the students but also from the teachers who should have known better, and the only reason was that Zaina didn't look like me.

That's men for you. And women. Look at poor tragic Zitface. The ultimate femme dyke in denial.

POLICE: You resented Zaina Abbour because of her relationship with Nero Adams and because she was outperforming you in academic work?

YM: Not enough to *kill* her if that's what you're implying. And nor did my dad before you start down that road. I never even told him what was going on. I just made sure I got homework extensions, individual after-school sessions; the teachers who liked me gave me tip-offs about what was coming up in tests and suddenly I was back in the running.

If I didn't know already, there was the clear proof that I had the sort of power that doesn't come through education.

I never imagined what it might lead to. Tabitha tried to warn me but I didn't listen. I thought I was God's gift. I mean, of *course* I did, right? Because people were always telling me I was. It took me quite a while to realize that was just an accident of genetics and the fact that I could contour.

It was all for nothing, though. Even with all the help I still couldn't do the difficult stuff, because when it came down to it I just didn't have the brains. Don't get me wrong, I'm OK, but I'm the kid aiming for the wastepaper basket from the front of the class.

POLICE: This was the wastepaper basket in the exam hall?

YM: (*sighs*) It's a metaphor. Look it up.

Anyway, the first two maths A-level papers were bad. I never let on, but I knew I had to do a blinder with Paper Three or not only was I not going to get the maths prize

(which would have been a massive joke by the way –
that was Zaina's all along), but I might not even get
the grades for med school. So I did what I always did. I
used my power.

Only it turned out I didn't have as much as I thought I did.
He did, though. And he was prepared to use it.

The Exam

10:00–10:15

Zaina slumps against the wall of the main building as the truth sinks in. She was wrong yet again. Ylsa had nothing to do with all this, she just couldn't cope with the exam.

Hadn't Zaina learnt her lesson with Saff? This whole thing has been a fairy tale, the product of her traumatized mind, as delusional as the excuses Poppy concocted for herself whenever a guy didn't message when he said he would: *he had no signal, he lost his phone, he was in an accident.* Anything rather than accept the truth. That she'd been deceived. And now Zaina has been doing exactly the same thing: deceiving herself. Desperate to believe the fanciful

219

tale Nero was spinning because it meant that they were connecting again.

That's it then. She's screwed herself and for no reason at all. Her rivals couldn't have planned this better if they'd got together and plotted it all out second by fucking second.

Hell, maybe they did.

I will destroy you.

Maybe there's a chance she could persuade Miss Zita to allow her to finish the exam, but she really can't face it. She's done. She just wants to go home and collapse on the sofa. She slides down the bricks to the warm tarmac of the path.

Apart from the seagull dozing on the science-block porch directly opposite her, she is alone in the silent college. It's as if the buildings are holding their breath, waiting for the storm of tears and self-recriminations. Because it's over. It's all over. Her dad put his faith in her and she failed him. Betrayed him in his last wish. Worst daughter. Cover yourself in ashes.

And yet for some strange reason she no longer feels the familiar weight of guilt. It's as if someone has reached down and lifted the dead albatross from round her neck.

Her reflection in the science-block door blinks at her, bewildered. Why doesn't she feel guilty any more?

Her thumb moves automatically across the dent in her finger, soothing the ache. The throbbing that has been there since the start of the exam has started to diminish. She looks down. The dent is softening, the flesh settling back. There is no longer any sign of her father's words cutting into her skin.

She blinks rapidly, taken aback by the new emotion coursing through her blood. Because now, instead of guilt, quickening her heart are the first stirrings of anger. Dropping her head back against the brick, she looks up into the blue sky.

It wasn't fair.

The sky gazes back at her, aloof and unreachable.

"It wasn't fair!" she shouts.

Her voice ricochets around the buildings and the seagull flaps away, ungainly in its shock.

"It wasn't fair." Her voice is softer now. "Your last words shouldn't have been *Make me proud*; they should have been…"

But now the tears come. She closes her eyes and lets them trickle out through her lashes. Because she can't blame him; she is just as bad. What her dad didn't say to her were the same words she didn't say to Nero that night under the pergola.

Like father, like daughter. When it came down to it, they had both been incapable of understanding what was really important. And out here, alone under the endless blue sky, she knows in her heart what that is. Knows it was her mum who was right all along, her tired, unassuming mum whose only talents seemed to be to make meals and clean the house and care for her children. *I love you … that's all that matters.*

Nero would have walked by her side through fire, they would have fought necromancers, lifted curses (even the sort of curses laid upon you by people who loved you); nothing could have separated them. Except her.

She tries to sense if he is close by. Sometimes she would do this and be right; she would be longing for him, and there he would be, ambling down the corridor of the hospital, curls bouncing in front of his eyes, rucksack slung over his shoulder, ready to work, or game or whatever she felt like doing. But now all she can sense is the sun on her eyelids, the wind in the plane tree and the dusty smell of summer traffic on the high road. She sighs and opens her eyes. Time to go home.

Struggling to her feet, as stiff as an old lady, she trudges back into the building and heads for the locker room. As she stumps down the stairs, she can hear a phone ringing but it stops before she enters the room.

Fetching her bag from the locker, she automatically glances through the door to where Nero was smoking when she arrived for the exam. Of course he isn't there. Why would he be? That was almost two hours ago. It seems almost unbelievable that's all it's been. She feels like a different person from the one who arrived at Franklyn this morning.

She swings the bag on to her back and it settles into the ridges in her shoulders, the way her father's pen settled into the dents in her fingers. She feels the familiar stab of panic, this time justifiably; she really *has* left the pen somewhere. She should go back and fetch it.

But instead she just stares into the cool darkness of her locker. On the door are scraps of the white sticker she picked off with her fingernails the Monday after Emily's party. Nero had stuck it there weeks before. It read: I WAS BRAVE AT THE DENTIST. He'd got it when he went in for a root canal as a consequence of an early Haribo addiction. She'd scratched it off in anger, but she had no right to claim bravery anyway. Because she isn't brave. When she was confronted with something scary, she ran away. Because love is scary. It makes you do things you don't want to, things that make you miserable.

No. She won't fetch the pen.

Pausing at the door to the stairs, she takes one last look at the place. She won't be back here again. This chapter of her life is over. No, not a chapter. It's a whole book, every plot strand finished too definitively for a sequel. A book with a disappointing ending that will just be slotted into the bookcase and forgotten about.

She turns to go through the door and then the phone starts ringing again.

She turns back, walks a few steps towards the locker bank.

The ringing is coming from locker 76. It's Chanelle's phone. In the shrill tone she can almost hear the panic of a worried parent who just keeps calling and calling their missing daughter because they don't know what else to do.

She frowns. People are still looking for Chanelle, and clearly no one has told them her phone is here in the school.

Is there a chance Chanelle posted something that

might reveal her state of mind or her plans? If so, her parents probably wouldn't have seen it, and since most of Chanelle's friends at Franklyn do maths, Zaina might be the only person who knows she's missing and also has access to her socials.

Crossing to the bench, she sits down, opens her bag and gets out her own phone.

She's so far behind with Instagram that the posts take ages to update. Images flicker past, whole lives flashing before her eyes, made up of hugs and laughs and dogs – so many dogs – and holidays and party dresses and brunches with friends, all the things she's missed out on for so long. Eventually she's up to date and can search for Chanelle's profile. Chanmanfan05's last Insta post is a picture of her dachshund, asleep, with its huge ears spread out on Chanelle's knees. But that was posted months ago, so it looks like Chanelle has been off socials as long as Zaina has.

She checks Snap. Chanelle hasn't shared any recent photos or videos, so there's no clue to her whereabouts, but Zaina should still let someone know that the phone is down here.

Her fingers hesitate as they're about to close the app.

With all the shouting and drama, Ylsa certainly gave the impression that she had left the school, but is it possible that was for Zaina's benefit? Should she check Ylsa really *has* gone?

She opens Snap Map and a hundred little bitmojis fill the screen. They are scattered all over the globe, from Vietnam to New York to South Africa – the lucky students who were whisked on holiday as soon as their exams finished – but the majority crowd around one place. She zooms in on the school.

Closer.

Closer.

She sees herself in the same crowded little spot as Poppy, Tabitha, Saff and the others.

Ylsa seems to be in the nail bar on the high street.

Of course, according to the app, Chanelle is still here, because her phone is.

But so is Nero.

She frowns and moves in as close as she can. He still seems to be in the science block. If so, wouldn't he have seen her leave the exam? But he hasn't tried to call her. What could he be doing in there? Has Mr Peters found him and given him a bollocking? Or has he actually found

Chanelle? If so, surely he'd have alerted someone and they'd have called her parents, so there wouldn't be any need to keep ringing her phone. Which must mean that Chanelle is still missing.

As if to prove this point, the phone in locker 76 starts up its anxious wail once more.

She sighs heavily. She's so tired. And not just physically; a bone-deep weariness makes her want to go home, go to bed and not wake up until September. The last thing she needs is a wild goose chase around the school looking for a frenemy who might (unlikely) or might not (highly likely) be unconscious in a toilet.

But she has no choice, because, right now, she may well be all Chanelle's got.

She gets to her feet and swings the bag on to her back. One last check through her workings to make sure she hasn't made a silly mistake and then that's it. She will walk out of this place for the last time.

Leaving the locker room, she tramps back up the stairs.

Outside, the school is still eerily quiet. Even the traffic on the high road seems muted on this baking day. The sky is an empty, endless blue. No one is looking down on her, judging her, wanting something from her.

The sudden sense of pressure falling away makes her dizzy.

She walks out of the shadow of the main building and into the sunshine.

Is it quiet enough that she would hear a conversation in the science block between Nero and Mr Peters? The windows are closed, but surely she would hear if there were raised voices. This may mean that Mr Peters is still searching the block and Nero is hiding from him. It's been ages since he left the exam, but the Snap Map said he was still there, so maybe Mr Peters is taking his time. She really doesn't want to risk running into the teacher and having to explain what she is doing and why.

She turns her head right to left, taking in the college grounds from the car park to the distant art and DT blocks. Where would *she* go if she didn't want people to know what she was doing? To be honest, she'd probably just hide out in her bedroom. But Chanelle clearly isn't in her bedroom.

Zaina's dark hair is like the black side of a Leslie cube, absorbing the throbbing heat of the sun peeking over the science block. It has drawn a dust-and-rubber smell from the asphalt roof of the nearby canteen.

The kitchen contains lots of bladed items.

Her heart drops. Suddenly this all feels very real.

She sets off, glancing nervously through the science-block windows as she goes. It's hard to see past the reflections but every room seems to be empty. There's another set of classrooms on the other side of the building, so perhaps Nero is in one of those, hiding out, staying quiet.

Her feet move quietly across the tarmac path, whispering against the browning grass growing up through the cracks. It's probably paranoia, but she feels watched all the way, as if someone is playing a big joke on her, giggling behind doors.

She comes to the drama block first. Pasted to the door is a scrappy poster for the department's production of *Macbeth*. It's been cheaply produced with stark white type on a black background half obscured by a slew of blood spatter.

She stops. The blood on her and Nero's exam papers was the catalyst for all this. But surely, after catching her trying to cheat, Miss Zita wouldn't have let Chanelle stay in M1 alone with the papers, especially if she was upset enough to hurt herself. That makes no sense. But, on the other hand, if she's hidden in a toilet somewhere, how did the blood get on the papers in the first place?

She stares at the poster. Has she got this all wrong?

The answer is yes, of course she has. Her behaviour since the beginning of the exam has been completely irrational and illogical. Instead of following the sensible path to success laid out for her by her dad, she has allowed Nero to lead her into one of his fairy tales. She's about to turn round when there is a flash in the glass of the door, a reflection of movement behind her.

She gasps and spins round.

The shadows are all perfectly still but she's certain she saw something. Could it be the seagull again, flying past the windows of the science block?

She can make out little apart from her own reflection and she squints to try to see through to the darkness beyond. Either the labs are empty or any occupant is standing so still they have merged into the geometric pattern of shadows inside.

"Nero?" she calls, probably too softly to be heard behind the glass.

But why would he be just standing there watching her? Her flesh prickles.

Get this over with quickly and then go home.

She hurries on, past the drama block to the canteen, relieved when she finds the door unlocked. Passing through the foyer, she enters the dining hall.

In the breeze from the opening door a KitKat wrapper rolls like tumbleweed across the grey lino. Without the bustle of students, the clinking of cutlery and crockery, the voices raised in amusement or annoyance, the place has a Chernobyl air of abandonment. Her footsteps echo around the empty tables and chairs as she makes her way towards the serving counter. The silver trays lined up along the counter gleam, cleaner than she has ever seen them. They're usually filled with the sort of cheap, slimy salad options you get in a Harvester.

She only realizes she is holding her breath when she reaches the counter and can see past to the kitchen area beyond. There is no pool of blood, no pair of legs protruding from behind the large stainless-steel island in the centre of the room. Above the island hangs a pan rack. One side of it is magnetized and stuck to this section is a line of kitchen knives. There don't seem to be any obvious gaps, but to be certain Chanelle isn't there, Zaina should check behind the island.

Lifting the hatch in the counter, she walks into the

kitchen. The place has a lingering smell of stale cooking oil and bins. There are no windows and without the fluorescent overhead lights the only illumination is the dull gleam from the stainless steel. Though she's fairly sure Chanelle isn't in here, her heart is in her mouth as she walks round the block dominating the middle of the room like a huge silver coffin.

She exhales. Nothing.

Because she's seen far too many thrillers, she slides open the metal doors of the island, but no body tumbles on to the red lino. The cabinet is filled with roasting trays and a dead spider lies on its back in the upper tray, legs in the air. She straightens up, casting her gaze around the room from this new angle, but there is no weeping Chanelle clutching her bloodied wrists. Of course there isn't.

Something buzzes and she jumps violently.

But it's just a message coming through. Swinging her bag on to the counter, she takes out her phone. She exhales. It's Nero.

I'm in the science block.

Did you find her? she replies quickly.

The message is seen but he doesn't respond.

                    Hello? Did you find Chanelle?
No.
                    Then what are you doing?
Having a cig. Come and meet
me and we can hang out.

Her heart pounds with anger. *Why is he being so fucking casual?* This wasn't all a ploy to get her on her own, was it? It had better bloody not have been.

Are you kidding?
                    Cmon. It'll be fun.
Fuck you.
                    Don't be like that.
Fuck you.

She experiences a head rush of rage. To think she was feeling remorse about him! She never wants to see or speak to him again. Turning her phone off, she stuffs it back in her bag. But as she's pulling the cords, she catches a flash of movement in the mirror of the prep table.

Her head snaps up. Beyond the service counter the dining hall is empty, the chairs and tables stretching all the way to the open door that leads back to the foyer and toilets. She forgot about the toilets; she should have checked them on the way in.

"Hello?" she calls softly. "Chanelle?"

It could have been the seagull again, she thinks doubtfully, or perhaps Mr Peters walking past the window. Her heart lurches, but if it was, he hasn't come in, so maybe the bright daylight made it difficult to see into the gloomy kitchen. Either way, it's a warning. She needs to get off the school premises before she ends up in big trouble. Slipping the dead phone back into her bag, she swings it over her shoulder.

Could it be Nero? Has he located her through Snap Map and come after her? But if so, why not show himself?

"Nero? If that's you, come out."

The silence thrums.

"This isn't funny, OK?

Her hand moves to the rack above the prep table and the carving knife gives a quiet plink as it detaches from the magnetic strip. "Nero? I mean it. Come out."

And then she feels very silly. A seagull flies past the

window and she thinks it's her former best mate coming to murder her? The knife gives a disapproving tut as she replaces it, then she picks up her bag and leaves the kitchen.

Both sets of toilets are empty and miraculously clean, smelling of bleach rather than their usual eau de stale urine. Stepping back out into the foyer, she sees, through the glass doors, the seagull, strutting up the tarmac walkway, its yellow beak curved into a smirk.

Before venturing back outside, she presses her face against the glass, trying to see as far as possible left and right. There is no sign of Mr Peters, Nero, Chanelle or even Ylsa. She half wishes she hadn't turned off her phone or she'd be able to check on all of them. Maybe she'd even find that Chanelle was on the move, on her way home – but she doesn't want to hang around waiting for it to start up and she certainly doesn't want it going off and alerting anyone to her presence – Nero *or* Mr Peters.

The door gives a treacherous squeal as she eases it open and steps back outside into the baking heat.

The prefabricated building to her left, furthest from the main block, houses the art and DT rooms. Should she even bother traipsing down there? There's a good chance they'll be locked up, considering the valuable equipment inside.

She sighs. She's here now, and the damage to her future is done, so she may as well follow this through. At least it delays the moment at which she has to go home and explain to Mum what she's done. And, worse, the flimsy reason for visiting such calamity on herself. *Nero told me to.*

Daddy did know best after all. When she gets the pen back, she'll stab it into her eyeballs a few times so that she's never again in danger of forgetting that fact.

It's only a couple of hours to midday and her shadow is short in front of her as she hurries towards the prefab. On the other side is a field that has been earmarked for two hundred council houses, but the companies that are supposed to be building them keep going bust. You get no signal out here, so she needn't have bothered switching her phone off.

Every few paces she feels compelled to turn back to check she isn't being observed, but it's hard to tell. Anyone following her could just dart between the buildings. Though why they would want to she can't imagine. Unless it is to get her alone out here, without a phone signal and too far for anyone to hear her scream.

This is a somewhat sobering thought but then her brow furrows. Nero isn't capable of anything like that. Then again, he's surprised her before.

Boys are only after one thing.

She glances behind her again, but the only movement is the slow creep of the traffic on the distant road.

Miraculously the art block is open. Stepping inside the foyer, she lets the door swing quietly shut behind her. She remembers her tour of the college before she joined and how impressed her mum was with the sophisticated work produced by the more creative members of the student body. Now she finds herself pinned to the spot by an enormous painting of an eye on the wall opposite the door, executed with such photorealism she can make out the tear ducts and each brilliant cyan thread of the iris. The colour of her dad's eyes before the cancer bled them yellow. The intense gaze does not so much as follow you round the room as swallow you up and it's an effort to tear her eyes away.

In, out, home.

No toilet here, only two sets of double doors with square windows. She takes the set on the left, into the DT room.

A scan of the room reveals nothing immediately out of

place. Moving between the tables, she inhales the lingering scents of sawdust and heated plastic. She has only been here once before when (for some reason that seemed extremely funny at the time) Nero wanted to 3D-print a plastic banana with his brother's face on.

The 3D printer is on a worktop in the corner, beside the machine and laser cutters. Fortunately there is no sign of a severed and neatly cauterized digit.

Not funny, she tells herself sternly. Nothing about this situation is funny; it's just an incredibly pointless way to throw away her future.

She gets to the end of the room, where the A-level projects have been neatly stacked against the wall. There are side tables and lamps, a children's ride-on train, a sledge, an intricately turned candlestick. Each item is beautiful and useful. Like maths, as her dad would have it, although here is beauty you can touch. She runs her hand down the flank of a chair that seems to have been made of a single sweeping sheet of wood. It looks like a person kneeling to pray. Presumably there are bladed items in the drawers under the worktables but if Chanelle came here for one, she has taken it away to use. There is no sign of another soul.

She heads back to the door.

The last place to check is the art room, and there aren't many weapons there, apart from scissors and textile needles, so it shouldn't take long. Averting her gaze from the giant blue eye as she crosses the foyer, she goes in.

The feel of this place couldn't be more different from the regimented desks of the maths classrooms; the only artwork on those walls being rules and formulas printed on rainbow-coloured paper in a craven attempt to make the dry subject matter seem more fun. *A pointless qualification,* her dad had said when she hinted that she might want to do art for GCSE. He had shown her some kind of league table on a newspaper website that told you that a career in the creative arts would leave you in poverty, so she'd taken computer science instead and spent her time learning about databases and Structured Query Language.

Here is another more magical world, a world of emotion rather than logic. There are mood boards and colour wheels, wooden mannequins twisted into impossible contortions. Paint is spattered with abandon on tables, walls, floors and even the ceiling. Draped like bunting from wall to wall are a series of etchings of the college buildings, with multicoloured washes. Each is attached with a bulldog clip to a white nylon cord in order to dry out. The yellow and blue ones make the college look airy and modern, but the red and purple washes give the place an almost gothic feel. The red paint has dropped on to the blue lino beneath, leaving stains the colour of old blood.

Propped up along the worktop on the other side of the room, leaning against the bank of windows, are still-life paintings of a bowl of apples. Some are as photorealistic as the eye in the foyer, some are more impressionistic and some are entirely abstract: the apples no longer green or round and not even 3D but flat and square and entirely wrong. Yet somehow right too, as if there is not a single answer to the problem of how to paint apples, but myriad answers. She blinks at the picture of the square blue apples, dazed. Imagine if you could simply *interpret* a question.

If, instead of *telling* her to make him proud, her father had *asked* her, *Will you make me proud?* Perhaps she might have come up with a different answer to the one she has been working out for the past six months. Perhaps it would have been: *I will make you proud by being happy.* Or maybe she would have explored the question in a more abstract way, like the square apples. Perhaps her response would have been: *I will show you how well you loved me by loving other people just as well. That will make me proud of us both.*

She leans heavily against a wooden table, its surface gouged and beaten like a craggy face. Good grief. Is this what art is? A square blue apple that can unlock your heart.

A movement beyond the line of windows catches her eye. She refocuses from the painting to the science block in the far distance. A cloud bank has come up so it's hard to make out, but she thinks someone is standing at the window at the end of the block. Slowly they raise their hand and wave at her. At least, she thinks that's what the movement is. It's hard to tell. It could have been beckoning.

Instinctively she drops to a crouch. It's a ridiculous thing to do, as Mr Peters would never have waved, so it has to have been Nero trying to get her attention. She breathes heavily, her heart pounding, not quite sure how she has come to be crouched on the floor of the art room among the pencil shavings, while the sensible students are busy not making a hash of their final A-level exam.

Then she frowns. *Meet me and we can hang out.*

It's a weird expression for Nero. In fact, the messages were not in his usual tone of voice at all. For a start they'd used punctuation.

Maybe it wasn't him at the window. Was the person even looking her way? Could they have been waving at someone approaching from the other direction? A teacher? *Chanelle?* Tentatively she gets to her feet. The figure at the window is gone and there is no one else in sight. It might never have been there, just a product of her jangled nerves.

Just get this over with and go home.

She peers behind stacks of canvases. Beside them is a large cabinet certainly big enough for a human body but it contains only clay pots wrapped in cellophane. Next to the cabinet is a door labelled KILN ROOM. The red paint from the etchings has made it over here too, seeming to spill out from under the door. But this paint glints in the sunlight. Fresh and wet.

Reaching forward, she grasps the handle and pulls opens the door.

The floor of the kiln room is awash with the red paint, and lying face down in the middle of it, like a drowned Ophelia, is Chanelle.

MX SAFF JACKSON

RECORDED INTERVIEW

Date: 27th June

Location: South Harrow Police Station

Time: 14:37

Conducted by officers from the Met Police

SJ: Can somebody please tell me what's going on? I've been sitting out there for hours. What's happened?

POLICE: That's what we're here to find out.

SJ: From me? I dunno how you're expecting to find

anything talking to me. The first thing I knew about anything was the sound of sirens when I was in the exam.

POLICE: The exam was over by then.

SJ: Not for me. I had to go out for medical reasons, so I got extra time at the end. Miss Iggle went to find out what was going on and I looked out of the window, but I couldn't see anything because the ambulance was in the way. Then Miss Iggle comes back up with one of your mob and then I'm brought here and I've been here ever since, so I know sweet FA about anything.

POLICE: How long had you and Chanelle Goldstein been seeing one another?

SJ: I don't know. A year and a bit? We're on a break at the moment, but— What's this got to do with me and Chanelle?

POLICE: Miss Goldstein was discovered at around ten thirty this morning in the art block of Franklyn Roberts Academy with severe injuries.

SJ: Wh-what? What kind of injuries?

POLICE: Sit down, please.

SJ: The blood. The blood on the path. Was that … was that Chanelle's?

POLICE: Possibly. Zaina Abbour suffered separate injuries.

SJ: *Separate injuries?* Zaina? What the fuck is going on?

POLICE: As I said, that's what we're trying to find out.

SJ: I'm not saying another word until you tell me what's happened to Chanelle. Is she OK?

POLICE: Miss Goldstein is badly injured but alive.

SJ: Badly injured how?

POLICE: The injuries may have been self-inflicted.

SJ: Oh my God, oh my God. It's my fault. This is my fault.

POLICE: Just to confirm, you are saying that the injuries suffered by Miss Goldstein were inflicted by you.

SJ: What? No! No, I didn't mean that at all. I love Chanelle! I would never hurt her. There was that one time but that was an accident.

POLICE: What time was that?

SJ: I was upset. I pushed Chanelle away and accidentally split her lip.

POLICE: What were you upset about?

SJ: Football. The football team, but I don't see what that's got to do with... Oh, wait, I get it. It's always the partner, right? You think I did this, whatever it is.

POLICE: We're keeping an open mind. Can you tell us your movements yesterday afternoon and evening?

SJ: Yesterday? I was at home cramming for the exam… Oh shit.

POLICE: What?

SJ: My parents were out. I haven't got anyone to give me an alibi. My phone, right? You'll be able to track the pings on my phone, won't you? Actually, you know what, none of this matters. I don't care if you think I did it or you don't. I just care about Chanelle. You asked me why it was my fault. Because I've been so wrapped up in my own shit recently that I wasn't there for her when she needed me. I knew she was stressed but I never imagined she'd do something like this.

POLICE: What was Chanelle stressed about?

SJ: What she was always stressed about. Work. She sets herself these crazy high standards that no one could ever keep up with. She had to be the best all the time. Hold on. If you think Chanelle tried to kill herself, then why am I even here? Why are you asking me about my movements last night? There's something else, isn't there? Something you're not telling me?

POLICE: As I said, we're keeping an open mind. There is a possibility that Miss Goldstein's injuries may *not* have been self-inflicted.

SJ: What are you saying? That someone else hurt her? That they, what, that they tried to kill her?

POLICE: Calm down, please, Saff. Sit down!

SJ: I have to see Chanelle! Let go of me! LET GO OF ME!

The Exam

10:15–10:20

Bursting out into the daylight, Zaina tries to scream for help, but she must be going into shock because she can't find the breath. She decides it's better to save what remains for the sprint to the science block. Nero's phone will be quicker to use than waiting for hers to come to life. They can call an ambulance, then she'll go back to Chanelle and he can run and find Mr Peters or Miss Zita.

Chanelle is alive. God knows how, with all that blood, but she had a pulse and moaned when Zaina touched her. Zaina hopes she was conscious enough to understand that she hasn't abandoned her but gone to get help.

She sets off at a blundering stagger, and the distance

spaghettifies, the focus pull of a horror film. She wants to break down and cry, but she can't because she owes it to Chanelle to be strong, so she grits her teeth and pushes forward, and the urge to give up is slowly replaced with anger.

Lying in the pool of blood beside Chanelle, next to a pair of textile scissors, there was a note.

I'll never be good enough.

It might have been the spirit writing of Zaina's own subconscious. All this time she and Chanelle had been going through exactly the same thing. They could have supported one another, comforted and reassured one another, but instead they had turned on each other like caged rats, snapping and snarling in their fear.

I'll never be good enough.

How dare the world ever make any of them feel like that?

As the amphetamine of rage courses through her blood, all vestiges of guilt are washed away, like bacteria under UV light. They don't owe anyone anything. What kind of narcissist gives someone life to glorify themselves? Her dad wasn't a narcissist. He was just sick and afraid and not thinking straight. She should have known that.

A shaft of sunlight breaks through the clouds and the air becomes suddenly more breathable. Her vision clears and her chest loosens. Her thighs are pumping beneath her and she flies the final few metres to the science-block porch.

Yes, she could go on to the exam room but Miss Zita would only do what she's going to – call an ambulance. Zaina doesn't need an adult to tell her what to do any more. They might pretend they know everything but they screw up just as much as the people they're supposed to be older and wiser than.

She bursts through the doors. "Nero!"

Her voice echoes down the empty corridor, flanked on either side by doors. There is a faint chemical smell in the air. "Nero, I've found her! Where are you?"

The echoes die away and there is no answer. Is he playing some kind of game with her?

She sets off down the corridor, kicking each door open as she goes. The labs are all pristine and deserted: neat rows of desks with their gas taps and tidy shelves. This building is like the rational hemisphere of a brain, in contrast with the wild, creative side of the art room. Cold calculation versus hot and messy emotion.

"Nero! Stop pissing around and come out!"

But as she gets to the last two doors, she is forced to accept that she was wrong. There is no Nero and no Mr Peters. She has wasted precious time when she could have simply run up to Miss Zita in the assembly room. She kicks open the penultimate door, the one to the room where the person seemed to be waving at her. It's empty.

There is one left: the chemistry lab at the back of the building. While the other doors stood half open or ajar, this one is properly closed. She turns the handle and it opens with a creak. These are fire doors so they're heavy.

The first thing she notices when she enters the room is that the chemical smell is much stronger in here. The second thing she notices is Nero lying motionless on the floor.

She screams his name and the world snuffs out.

MR JONATHAN PETERS

RECORDED INTERVIEW

Date: 28th June
Time: 12:17
Location: King George's Memorial Hospital
Conducted by officers from the Met Police

POLICE: Your medical team have advised us that you sustained a serious head injury, so we will take this interview slowly, and if you feel unwell at any point, we can take a break.

JP: I just need to know about my students. Are they OK?

POLICE: They are in intensive care.

JP: They might die?

POLICE: The next few hours are critical. If you're able, it would be very helpful if you could share with us your recollections of what happened yesterday morning.

JP: I'll do my best. But my head...

POLICE: We'll try to keep it short. Let's start with what you were doing in the science block. According to your colleague, you were supposed to be invigilating the exam.

JP: One of the students left midway through. Later on I saw that he was still on school grounds, so I thought I'd better check on him. We've had some problems recently with students self-harming and I was worried that he might be having a mental health crisis. This period is so stressful for them all. I was searching the school when I saw one of his friends entering the science block. I figured maybe she'd arranged to meet him there, so I went after her. When I stepped inside the block I smelled the gas straight away and immediately realized the danger.

POLICE: Why?

JP: Nero Adams was a smoker. It's a no-smoking college but he never was one to respect the rules. I figured that if he was stressed enough to walk out, he might try to calm his nerves with a cigarette. If he lit up, he would ignite the gas.

I hurried down the corridor, opening the doors as I went. Then I heard a voices from the chemistry lab at the back of the building. I sprinted there, kicking open the door. And that's the last thing I remember before the explosion.

POLICE: Explosion?

JP: Sorry?

POLICE: There was no explosion.

JP: Then how did I get this injury?

POLICE: That's what we wanted to speak to you about.

The Exam

10:20–10:30

Zaina's eyes flutter open. She's lying on her back on the chemistry-room floor.

The chemical smell is gas and at first she wonders if there's been an explosion, but the room is not in any disarray. Maybe she just blacked out. But how could the gas have overcome her so quickly, and why did she wake up again so fast? Gas rises, so maybe the clear air underneath it revived her. Who knows? She never was much cop at chemistry.

The same thing must have happened to Nero too, but he clearly banged his head on the way down, knocking himself out. As she turns her head to look at him a bolt of pain shoots across her temples. She raises her fingers to her scalp. They come away bloody.

Nausea washes over her and she closes her eyes and waits for it to pass. In the silence she can hear the low hissing of the open gas tap. She needs to get up and turn it off.

As the wooziness recedes, she opens her eyes. Nero is lying beside her, the hand thrown out beside him resting in a pool of his own blood, his dark eyelashes completely still on his cheek. On the side of his head is a deep curved wound, like a toothless red grin, and his normally olive skin is sickly grey. But she can hear the rasp of his breathing. He's alive. And so is Chanelle. She has to get him out of here and get help for both of them. But she feels so bad herself she'll never have the strength to drag him out.

Perhaps if she finds her bag, she can manage to turn her phone on and summon help. Although you're not supposed to use any electronic equipment in a gas leak because of sparks. She'll just have to try to crawl outside.

She takes some deep breaths, preparing herself. The gas makes her gag. How can he not have smelled it when he came in? Or heard the hiss of the tap if he was here alone? He texted her so his phone didn't set off an explosion.

With a grunt of effort, she struggles up on to her elbows and pauses, gasping for breath.

There is a loud clang.

Turning her head in the direction of the sound, she has to blink a few times before the figure in front of her resolves itself into the tall frame of Mr Peters.

Thank God.

"Sir … there's been an accident… Nero…" It's an effort to speak and her head is throbbing so hard she can't think straight.

At the teacher's feet is a heavy-duty Bunsen burner stand. Did he drop it? Was that what made the clanging sound? But why was he holding a Bunsen burner stand in the first place? The frown sends pain lacerating between her temples.

She takes a deep breath and struggles to sit up. Mr Peters makes no attempt to help, only stares at her, his face bone white but for a smattering of dark freckles. He must be in shock at finding his students like this.

"I'm OK, Sir … but we need … to get Nero out of here…" She pauses, panting from the effort of speaking. "And then … get help … for Chanelle. She's hurt too."

Now, at last, he moves, but instead of hurrying to her side the teacher turns round to face the bench. He's turning the gas off.

Wait, no he isn't. There's the sound of a drawer sliding open. They don't keep medical supplies in these drawers, do they? As far as she knows it's only lab equipment.

When he turns back, he's holding something long and thin. "You shouldn't have come after him."

Zaina squints, trying to make out the object, but her vision is still swimming.

"You should have stayed in the exam."

"N–Nero," she croaks. "I came after Nero … because of Chanelle…"

"I didn't want to hurt Chanelle and I don't want to hurt you either, but what am I supposed to do?"

Her mouth opens and closes as she tries to make sense of this question; her brain is too foggy, but her vision has started to clear and now she can make out what it is he's holding: one of the clickers they use to light the Bunsen burners.

"Sir … be careful…" The gas is still on. If his finger slips, he might ignite it.

But it can't be the gas that made her collapse because her

head is beginning to clear. Her thoughts start to connect again, catching up.

I didn't want to hurt Chanelle…

What is he talking about?

I don't want to hurt you…

Why isn't he trying to help them?

"I have a family for Christ's sake!" the teacher mutters urgently almost to himself. "They need me." He rakes the fingers of his free hand across his face and through his hair. The perfect glossy chestnut hair that used to glow in the afternoon sunshine in last-period maths. Nero was convinced he stood by the window deliberately. When he takes his hand away, Zaina sees that his freckles have smeared.

None of this makes any sense.

"Don't you think I wish it could have ended with Chanelle? If it wasn't for fucking Nero…"

She blinks in surprise, even after everything that's happened, at the strangeness of a teacher swearing.

"But what choice do I have?" He starts backing away round the worktop and for a moment the stainless steel casts a beam of light across his face, painting the smeared freckles red.

Not freckles. Blood.

The same freckles spatter the Bunsen burner stand on the floor. Did he … did he hit them with it?

And now he's holding a lighter in room full of gas.

"Mr Peters," she croaks.

"The blast will knock you out," he says almost plaintively. "You won't feel a thing."

A surge of adrenaline gives her the strength to shout. "What are you doing?!"

He shakes his head rapidly, as if trying to repel an irritating insect and that's when she realizes he's actually going to do this. He reaches the door and glances behind him, out of the round window.

"It's almost ten thirty. Everyone will start coming out of the exam soon. I'm sorry, Zaina, really I am. But what choice do I have now, really? You'd do the same in my shoes…" And, with that, he passes through the heavy door and out of the gas-filled room.

Zaina stares in horror as the door clumps shut behind him, but there's nothing she can do.

Or, at least, only one thing.

She rolls over to face Nero. "Please, Nero, wake up." There's a different tone to her voice now. Not the urgency of survival – it's too late for that now – but a different kind of urgency. To correct the terrible mistake she made a month ago at Emily Blackwater's party.

Now, at last, his lashes flutter and rise and she is looking into the gold-flecked pools of his eyes, closer than they have been since that night in Emily's garden, that night when she took his beautiful words and made them ugly. She reaches up and cups his pale cheek with her hand. His eyes are still glassy and unfocused. Perhaps he is past understanding but this is the last chance she will ever have.

But she's out of time.

There is a loud bang.

The Day Before the Exam

16:45

Jonathan had almost completed his task when there was a clicking sound from the direction of the door.

He hadn't told Ylsa to meet him here, but she knew what he was doing – she'd *asked* him to do it – so maybe she'd come to surprise him. A grin spreading across his face, he crossed the room and opened the door for her.

He was surprised all right.

The stirring between his legs subsided at once.

Chanelle Goldstein stared at him, the credit card she was using to try to jemmy the worse-than-useless lock gripped in her white-knuckled hand. Her face, surrounded by its halo of red curls, slowly drained of blood. She was a bright girl. Too bright to be doing what she was doing, and her expression of horror suggested she knew exactly what this meant for her future.

Jonathan's panic began to subside. She thought *she* was the one in trouble.

He didn't need to make up any excuse as to what he was doing here. He was an adult in a position of authority. It hadn't even crossed her mind to wonder if he was up to something he shouldn't be. Frowning gravely, he gestured to the chair on the other side of the table. "I think we need to have a little chat, don't we, Chanelle?"

Head bent, she shuffled into the room and sank down into the chair.

"Are you going to report me, Sir?" Her voice wavered.

"This is very serious. Very serious indeed." He must make her work to persuade him to let her off. It couldn't seem too easy. "You came here to access the papers, didn't you? That's cheating, Chanelle."

"You are totally within your rights to go to the head, Sir" – she took a shuddering breath – "but if you do, then I'm … I'm so screwed. All the universities will have to be informed, won't they?"

"I imagine so."

"Will my other marks be cancelled? Will I have to—" She broke off with a sob.

He let the silence stretch, pretending to think, enjoying the sense of power. Then he sighed wearily, as if he had come to a reluctant conclusion. She would be quaking in her shoes, expecting the worst, and then when he delivered her from the jaws of her own personal hell – *Don't do it again and we'll say no more about it* – she would be overcome with gratitude. He paused a minute longer, fantasizing about how she might express that level of gratitude.

It was then he saw that he had made a mistake.

He should have cleared up before he went to the door, because as he moved towards the desk he saw her grey eyes taking in the open question paper, the calculator, the list of figures on the plain sheet of paper. Her brow furrowed.

Snatching up the exam paper, he dropped it into the box on the floor, then folded the sheet he was copying the answers on to and tucked it into his pocket.

But it was too late.

She raised her eyes and met his gaze. There was a new expression in them. Realization and a certain boldness. When she spoke her voice was steady. "I'm so sorry, Mr

Peters. You're obviously really busy. Maybe … um … we could just forget all about this."

His heart beat faster. She knew.

"I think we'd better have some privacy, don't you?" he said, moving back towards the still-open door.

As he approached the doorway, he heard something: a rhythmic squeaking dying away, but there was no time to contemplate this because something had caught his eye. A flash at the edge of his vision. He glanced back. Chanelle was sitting perfectly still and staring straight ahead, just as he had left her, but looking more closely, he saw her right hand moving in the bag on her lap. A square of light glowed through the fabric. She was messaging someone.

If she were to tell anyone what she'd seen, he was well and truly fucked. They would want to know why he'd been copying the paper. It would all come out. He'd got away with it last time. The benefits of being a popular teacher and a good-looking one: your colleagues were all too eager to believe that the student had made it up.

Kids these days, they had commiserated when he had handed in his resignation. *A bad grade or rejected advances and they'll turn on you, pull the #MeToo card. It's woke culture gone mad.*

But the powers-that-be wouldn't be so fast to dismiss a second accusation. It would probably spell immediate dismissal and a teaching ban for life. Vicky would definitely divorce him this time. Plus, Ylsa's dad was a fucking gangster so he'd probably end up in pieces in the estuary. *Holy shit.*

He had to stop her.

It was pure instinct. He lunged forward, grasped a fistful of Chanelle's auburn curls and yanked her head back. She gasped as their eyes met, and then he slammed her head forward on to the corner of the table.

After the crack there was complete silence.

Shit, shit, shit. What had he done?

Was she fucking dead?

Her forehead rested on the table, as if she'd simply fallen asleep in class.

Then he saw that her back was expanding and contracting. The relief brought tears to his eyes. He sank down into the seat opposite.

He should call an ambulance. He took out his phone, then hesitated. When she came round and told everyone, he would be finished.

Might she forget? A head injury would do that, right?

He googled it.

Yes, there was a good chance she would. And if she didn't, it would be his story – she tripped and bumped her head – against hers. Should he just go, make her wonder whether he was ever there at all? Hatcher saw him leave, after all. He made a big deal of it deliberately, asking about her daughter's new job and pretending to be interested in the answer, then whistling as he went to the car. He parked streets away and came back into the school via the field at the back of the art block.

Maybe she wouldn't even come round. Perhaps even now blood was filling her cranial cavity, putting pressure on her brain, shutting it down. Yes, that was the best solution. Leave now. Vicky would give him an alibi. She'd probably been asleep all afternoon anyway because of the baby, so wouldn't have a clue what time he came in.

He got up. Then froze.

That little bitch from his last school had seen him and Ylsa together in the art block. He'd thought they were being so careful. It was separate from the main school and what normal teenager liked hanging out somewhere with no phone signal? If Chanelle was found in the room with the exam papers, there would be all sorts of questions.

Tabitha Jain might come forward and tell what she'd seen. That wouldn't look good for his credibility, not good at all.

Keep calm. Chanelle was still unconscious. He had time to think.

The arm hanging limp by her side was criss-crossed with scars. She was on the watch list for pupils with mental health problems. Surely it was feasible that the pressure of exam season could push her over the edge, and if she was resorting to cheating, then she really must be stressed. Stressed enough to do *something stupid*, as they like to term it? Yes, conceivably.

Lifting her up, he saw a trickle of blood running down from her left nostril. He cleaned every trace of it from her face and the few specks that had dropped on to the table, using his own hanky, which he could dispose of on his way home, in the canal maybe.

As he carried her limp body out of the room, his shoes squeaked quietly on the lino and a horrible thought struck him. *That* was the sound he heard after Chanelle came in. Feet moving away down the corridor. Someone *saw* Chanelle coming into this room. And if he didn't find out who that was, he was in bigger trouble than he could ever have imagined.

One thing at a time. He must get her to the art room. It was far enough away from everywhere else that she wouldn't be found in a hurry, and there would be plenty of sharp objects a suicidal pupil could use to end their pain. Two deep cuts into her radial arteries and she might bleed out before she even regained consciousness. He could even leave a note, copying her handwriting from the books in her bag.

As the handsome teacher hurried away down the corridor, he couldn't help but notice how all that gym work to impress Ylsa meant that carrying a body barely broke him out in a sweat.

MISS POPPY CAMERON

RECORDED INTERVIEW

Date: 27th June
Location: South Harrow Police Station
Time: 13:23
Conducted by officers from the Met Police.

POLICE: Hello, Poppy. I'm aware you've had a nasty shock, but it's important that we try to establish what happened this morning and at the moment you're the only one who was present at the scene who's in a fit state to speak to us.

(*PC nods*)

POLICE: I know you spoke to the first responders, so I'd like you to tell me everything you told them, please, adding any more details that you can remember as you go. Would that be OK?

PC: Yes.

POLICE: In your own time then.

PC: Um, well … it was our last maths exam today, which I guess you know. It must have been … about halfway through the exam when I realized that something was going on between Nero and Zaina. Have you heard anything more about them? Are they going to be OK?

POLICE: We've had no word from the hospital as yet, but they are receiving the best care possible. All you can do now is help us and their families understand what happened.

PC: Well, a little way into the exam Nero just gets up and leaves. I assume he and Zaina have had some kind of a falling-out and he can't handle the stress of everything.

POLICE: Any idea what that falling-out might have been about?

PC: He would never have hurt Zaina if that's what you're implying. It was just … it was… Look, it doesn't matter. What matters is he's left, but Zaina's still acting strange and eventually Zitface – sorry, Miss Zita – she notices. I'm worried that Zaina's about to be thrown out, so I create a distraction. It works and Miss Zita forgets about Zaina so she can get on with finishing the paper. I know how important this is for her and that's why I'm so surprised that a few minutes later, like a full half-hour before the exam finishes, Zaina gets up and leaves too.

Has she gone to meet Nero? I think. Would she really throw away her mark for that? But if so, there's nothing I can do. I can't go after her cos I'm the last person she'll want to see.

POLICE: Why's that?

PC: I'll get to that. Anyway, I just carry on with my work. Now, I know you're supposed to use all the time you have in an exam, but when I get to the end of the paper

I decide to just leave. The whole thing has shaken me up and brought back some stuff that happened recently and I want to go home. So I leave my paper on the table, pick up my pencil case and walk out.

POLICE: If I'm understanding correctly, there was a falling-out between you, Zaina and Nero. It's important for us to know about that as it might give us some insight into the reasons for today's events.

PC: You'll understand if you let me finish.

So, anyway, in the stairwell there's this big window that looks out over the main path and the science block, and that's when I see Zaina. She's running up from the direction of the art block and she looks terrible. Upset and scared, and it seems like she has blood on her hands. Like I said, Nero would never, *ever* hurt her, so I figure maybe she fell over or something and she's going home, but instead of carrying on towards the gates, she ducks into the science block. I think that maybe she's meeting Nero there but the blood bothers me. I need to know she's OK – she was literally my best friend in the whole world, you know, and even after everything that happened I still care about her.

I make a split-second decision. Running down the stairs, I go out of the main block and follow her.

Coming in from outside the science building is really dark and I have to wait for my eyes to adjust. As I stand there in the gloom, I'm wondering again what the hell I'm doing. Whatever's going on, shouldn't I just leave them to it? By interfering am I going to wreck their relationship a second time? Then I hear his voice coming from one of the rooms at the far end. That decides me. They're together. I need to leave them alone.

I turn round, then I stop. Because the voice didn't sound like Nero.

I move a little bit further up the corridor and then I recognize the voice. It's Mr Peters.

Is Zaina in trouble? I think. But he doesn't sound angry or anything, so I figure that maybe he's trying to calm her down from whatever's upset her.

I guess, thinking back, I start to feel like there's something wrong when I still can't hear Zaina. I go nearer, sliding along the wall as quietly as I can. That's when I first smell gas. It gets stronger as I get closer, but then I forget about it, because now I can make out what Mr Peters saying. It's about not wanting to hurt them.

POLICE: Them?

PC: Her and Chanelle. That's what he says.

I'm pretty sure I've misheard and I almost turn round and leave, but then I think of … of what I did to my best friend, how I betrayed her, and how even if I'm about to make a colossal fool of myself, and maybe piss Zaina off even more, I have to make sure she's OK. I take a deep breath, tiptoe up to the door of the chemistry lab and peer through the window.

And then I just stare.

Nero and Zaina are lying on the floor.

Nero is out cold but Zaina is still conscious, though now there's blood running down her face as well as on her hands.

For ages my brain just doesn't compute what I'm seeing, and if Mr Peters were to turn his head a fraction, he'd see me standing there with my mouth open. But he's still talking, and what he says then… Well, my brain is stuttering like … like a system malfunction. A voice in my head is saying, *You must have misheard. Mr Peters is such a nice guy.* Because he's talking about … about killing them.

You can be so floored when something goes against what you're expecting, can't you? It's like a trick question; you think you know what you're supposed to do and you almost get caught out. And I almost did, because just then he turns round. Our faces are right opposite each other, with just the glass of the window between them, but he looks through me, as if all he can see is his own reflection.

In the second I have before he opens the door, I duck into

the lab opposite. With my back against the wall, I can't see what's going on, so I creep back and peer through the crack.

Peters is standing in the corridor looking down at something in his hand. It's a Bunsen burner lighter.

He takes a step over to the door of the lab that's filled with gas, where my best friends are lying, and he opens the door and brings the hand holding the lighter up to the gap.

And then I realize I'm just standing there waiting for him to kill my friends, and finally my brain starts working again.

The chemistry labs all have fire extinguishers. There's one on the wall beside me. I just have to pull it out of its holder. It clinks as I do it and that's enough to catch his attention. He starts to turn.

I guess I've always been impulsive. I never stop to think through the consequences of my actions. Like sleeping with the boy my best friend is in love with… So anyway, I realize now I have no idea how to work a fire extinguisher.

I'm fiddling frantically with the nozzle as he starts coming towards me.

He kicks the door fully open, then he steps into the room and his face is twisted and ugly. He's going to drag me into the room with my friends, and then he'll click the lighter and we'll all be dead.

That's when I give up trying to work the fire extinguisher and I swing it sideways, like a cricket bat.

The boom as I slam it into his head echoes down the corridor.

THE FRANKLYN ECHO

Voice of Your Community   30th June

LOCAL TEACHER CHARGED WITH ATTEMPTED MURDER AFTER TEENS LEFT FIGHTING FOR LIFE

A maths teacher at Franklyn Roberts Academy Sixth Form College has been arrested following a serious incident at the school on the morning of 27 June.

Three teenagers were rushed to hospital after a fourth raised the alarm at around ten thirty. Two are in a critical condition with serious head injuries and knife wounds. The injuries of the third were said to be serious but not life-threatening.

Married father of one Jonathan Peters, 34, is being questioned over the attempted murder of the unnamed teenagers, who were believed to be sitting an A-level examination at the time of the attacks, but police have warned the charges may become more serious if the condition of the victims were to worsen.

It has come to light that a complaint was made about

Peters during his time at a previous school, where he allegedly entered into a relationship with a female pupil. The complaint was dismissed and he voluntarily left his post shortly afterwards.

Our source tells us that Peters claims the injuries sustained by his pupils were a result of self-harming and a gas-related accident. When asked to comment on this, Detective Constable Oliver Browning described Peters claims as "utter bollocks". You can follow the developments on this story, including updates on the condition of the young victims, on our website.

Two Months Later

8:30–10:30

Zaina wakes early. It's not even five and the dawn light forms rippling patterns over the ceiling, as if she's lying underwater. She doesn't jump out of bed to take advantage of the extra revision time or panic that she'll lose concentration in the exam, she just lies there, watching the light change and strengthen, sharpening the outlines of the furniture, making everything clearer. After a while the birds start to sing, and a little later she hears Heli calling for Mum.

She gets up then. She wants to be with them.

Pausing in the kitchen doorway, she smiles. Her mother and her baby sister are getting on with their lives. Heli doesn't think about what she's lost; she isn't fearful of the future. She lives in the precious moment: like this one, her tongue pushed out as she concentrates on the important task of finger-painting her face with bean juice. If Zaina had studied Heli more and her revision books less, maybe she'd have learned something valuable.

Mum finishes chopping apple into little pieces and turns round. She gives a dramatic gasp and clutches her face as she catches Heli in the act. "It's a bean monster!"

For a second, when Heli laughs, she turns into Dad. A baby Dad sent back to the start for a reboot.

"Morning," Zaina says from the doorway.

Mum looks up and her smile stutters. Zaina knows she's worried about how today will go, and she can't really blame her. "Morning, peanut. How are you feeling?"

"Fine."

Mum looks better these days. Better than the new widow with the scooped-out eye sockets. Better than the terrified mother running into the hospital in June, wild-haired, Heli screaming on her hip, the boys pale and uncharacteristically obedient. When the doctors told her that Zaina was going to be just fine she cried harder than she did when Dad died.

Afterwards, when Auntie Patsy had picked up the

kids, they had the first alone time for as long as Zaina could remember.

"I hate this bloody hospital," Mum had said in a hushed voice, though they were in a private room. "If I never set foot in the damned place again, it'll be too soon."

Zaina agreed. It was all so drearily familiar: the white walls, the metal bin, the paper dispenser, the trolley table, the plastic chair, the remote control that did various things to the bed, none of which made a terminally ill man feel any more comfortable.

"When your dad died, I was actually relieved that we were done with the place. Took me a while to forgive myself for that one, I can tell you. The guilt." She shook her head ruefully.

At that Zaina had burst into tears.

Mum pulled her into her arms, and when Zaina was ready to speak she told her about the promise. About the despair of not being able to live up to it. Of knowing you would always be a disappointment.

For a while Mum didn't say anything. In the past, if she had a question, Zaina would always go to her dad. She thought because he was always the first to speak that meant he was cleverer than her mum, but now she was starting to realize that Mum took longer to answer because she thought about things more deeply.

"I get that you venerate your dad," Mum said slowly. "It's easy to make saints out of the dead. But he wasn't a saint, and he wasn't right about everything. He was wrong to make you feel you owed him anything. Life isn't a gift that you have to repay your parents for; it's a huge liberty that we inflict on you all for our own selfish reasons. Your job is not to make us proud; it's to make yourselves happy."

"But that's how you get happiness, Mum," Zaina said weakly. "Doing well at school, getting a good job, making money…"

Mum smiled. "You think money stops you worrying? You think there's no divorce or illness or depression among the rich? Money buys you *things*, baby; happiness comes from somewhere else entirely, and if I could tell you how to get it, then I'd be a billionaire. But I do know it won't come from working yourself into the ground. There's so much more to life. The beautiful world we live in. Family, friendship, love."

Love. She made it sound so easy.

"How's your head?" Mum says, as Zaina enters the kitchen.

"Fine."

"Good. Can you manage some breakfast?"

"I'll get it."

Opening the cereal cupboard, Zaina automatically reaches for the muesli: slow-release carbs that will keep her energy levels up throughout the exam. But at the last minute she pulls out the boys' Coco Pops instead. Christ, she loves Coco Pops. The price of the deliciousness will be a sugar crash and savage hunger pangs in about an hour's time, but fuck it. She'll take the short-term pleasure over long-term good sense. Dad is proof that you never know if you're going to get a long term anyway.

As she eats, she feeds Heli the odd chocolate puff and lets her drink some of the chocolate milk from the bowl, and then it's time to get ready.

Gathering her exam materials together, she realizes the fountain pen only has a quarter of a cartridge worth of ink. It's unlike her not to be better prepared, but there's no helping it now. She'll just have to use a black rollerball like everybody else. She removes the precious pen from her pencil case and lays it carefully down on the desk. The gold inscription catches the morning light and dissolves into a white blur. It was good of Miss Zita to rescue it for her. She even delivered it to the hospital with a bunch of roses.

"Right, I'm off," Zaina calls, walking out into the hallway.

There is a moment's hesitation and then her mum calls back, "OK, see you later."

Zaina smiles. She knows her mum's deliberately trying not to make a big deal of the exam, but she really doesn't have to worry. Zaina doesn't care. She really doesn't. Her first-choice uni knows what's happened and has given her a reduced offer, one which she's likely to hit even if she scores a zero for this paper. And when it comes to the maths prize, she finds it hard to relate to the person that ever wanted it. None of them do; they've talked about it on the WhatsApp group they created in the aftermath of the last exam. It's called The Magic Number because there are three of them.

Her, Ylsa and Chanelle.

Chanelle survived Peters' attack because, even as she drifted in and out of consciousness, she was clever enough to realize she needed to put pressure on the wounds. Rolling on to her stomach and pressing her body weight on to her arms did not stop the blood loss but slowed it enough that she survived until Zaina found her. Or until Poppy saved them all, actually. Chanelle's doing surprisingly well, considering. Maybe because she's back with Saff.

Letting herself out of the flat, Zaina walks down the stairs, in and out of the bars of light falling through the windows of the stairwell. It reminds her of Nero. A lot of things do.

It's a beautiful cloudless morning, like the last time they sat this exam, only less stifling, as if even God wants to resit the day and try to do it better. The bus arrives quickly and she spends the journey listening to her playlist. The streets scroll past and songs start and end, until at last there are some familiar bars of piano.

"*She'd take the world off my shoulders*," begins the singer, but it's Zaina's stop, so she won't be able to listen to the end.

The sun is so bright by now that when she gets off the bus a bolt of pain shoots through her head and she leans against the shelter to let it pass. The doctor said she might have headaches for a while. He also said she might struggle to concentrate, but the truth is, she hasn't really tried. She's played with Heli and lounged in the park with Poppy, who's still acting ridiculously grateful, despite *literally* saving everyone's life.

293

A car growls up to the kerb in front of her.

"You OK?"

She opens her eyes, squinting through the pain.

Ylsa is leaning out of Tabitha's battered Honda Civic. The old Ylsa wouldn't have been seen dead in such an old banger, but Ylsa's princess polish has mostly rubbed off. She's cut her blonde mane into a sharp bob and let the roots grow through: less maintenance for her September plans. Turns out she's not going to be a doctor after all, at least not for a while. She's going travelling in South America with Tabitha – proper travelling, with backpacks and crappy hostels and poor hygiene, much to her dad's chagrin.

Zaina knows this because they're friends now. Real friends.

And here comes her other friend, walking along the pavement hand in hand with Saff, who can't be persuaded to leave Chanelle's side for longer than a few minutes these days.

"I'll wait in Maccy D's," Saff says as the pair join Zaina, before kissing Chanelle's cheek and crossing the road.

Telling Tabitha she'll walk the rest of the way, Ylsa gets out of the car and the Honda putters off.

"Morning," Zaina says, smiling at her friends.

"So what do we think today?" Ylsa says. "Zitface pulls off her human skin and dissolves us with her death ray?"

"A wormhole opens up and we fall through to a parallel universe," Chanelle says, "where A stars get you the electric chair."

Ylsa rolls her eyes. "Boring."

"You're right," Chanelle says. "We've set the exam-experience bar pretty high."

The three of them walk through the gates of Franklyn Roberts Academy.

Seeing the college for the first time since it all happened, Zaina doesn't know what she expected to feel, but it's not this: a kind of detached recognition. She spent two of the most eventful years of her life here – her father died, she fell in love, someone tried to murder her – but that all seems part of the distant past now.

There are just two cars in the car park. The college will be sticking rigidly to the two-invigilator rule during this exam, and no one will be going to the toilet alone.

The grass growing up through the path has browned and rustles beneath their feet as they walk towards the door of the main building. Ylsa pulls it open and Zaina is about to follow her through to the dim interior but Chanelle pauses, her eyes fixed on the distant art block.

"You all right?" Zaina says.

"It's strange," Chanelle says softly. "In a way I'm grateful for what happened. It taught me something. There are people out there who mean you harm but there are people that care too. People who think you're worth something." She flicks a shy smile at Zaina, absently passing a hand over her forearm. She wears short sleeves these days.

Zaina moves her own hand to the side of her head. There is a neat purple line, like an extra parting, from where the Bunsen burner stand split her scalp.

"Come on," Ylsa mutters from the bottom of the stairs. "Zitface is waiting."

Miss Zita smiles as they join her on the landing, apparently unconcerned at having to come back into school a full week before the beginning of term.

She hugs them one by one, and when she pulls away Zaina sees that her eyes are shining. Maybe even Zitface has been changed by what happened in June.

"Right, ladies. Let's hope today goes a little more uneventfully, shall we?" Her thin lips bend into an uncharacteristic smile.

As she turns, the girls exchange glances – *who is this woman and where's Miss Zita?* – and follow the teacher through the red door and down the corridor.

It's never happened before – students missing out on an exam due to someone trying to murder them. The exam board tried to get them to accept a predicted grade, but Ylsa's dad threatened to take them to court. To be fair, nobody had actually tried to kill Ylsa, she just couldn't do the paper, but as the victim of Peters' grooming, her year had been pretty fucked too.

They arrive at the door of the assembly room.

The three desks are sitting in a line in the middle of the room. Zaina will be at the back, where she always is, but for the first time Nero won't be working beside her.

"OK?" Chanelle murmurs.

She smiles and nods, then she takes a deep breath and crosses the threshold. Mrs Hatcher is opening the last window, and the room is cooler than last time, so there shouldn't be any risk of fainting. At the memory Zaina smiles to herself. Poppy offered to come with her today but she said no. It was Poppy that dealt with the aftermath of everything, turning off the gas, summoning help, constantly terrified that Peters might come round and flee the scene or attempt to finish what he'd started. All the while Zaina crouched on the floor of the chemistry lab and begged Nero to wake up.

Later, in the hospital, Peters invoked his right to silence, but the police think there's more than enough evidence to convict him without a confession. Forensics found Chanelle's blood on a shirt in a skip near his house, and handwriting experts confirmed the note had been written by him. The blood on the papers was also found to be Chanelle's. No one knows how it got there but it's firm evidence that she was in Room M1 the night before the exam. Until the trial Peters will be twiddling his thumbs in Wandsworth prison.

"Sit down, girls," Miss Zita says.

Zaina takes her place. She is a little further away from the windows so she can't see down to the path but she can just make out the science-block roof if she cranes her neck. The football still lies, deflated, on a cushion of moss burned brown by the long hot summer.

She looks down at the paper in front of her. *Mathematics Paper 3.*

There's a single blemish in the margin halfway down, but when she runs her finger across it, it doesn't smudge.

"Seeing as we're not waiting for anyone else, we can start a little early, so please fill in your name and candidate number."

Zaina opens her pencil case and takes out a black rollerball. She hasn't picked up a pen in two months and there are no longer any indentations on the sides of her fingers for it to tuck into, only patches of slightly calloused skin, like a healed battle scar.

"Now I know it's a beautiful day and you've probably all got plans, but don't leave as soon as you finish. Take the time to check through your paper and make sure you haven't made any mistakes."

As she writes her name and candidate number, Zaina is acutely aware of the empty expanse of parquet stretching away to her left.

"Right, ladies. You may begin."

Zaina works solidly through the paper. Most of the time she remembers the methods, but with some questions she draws a blank. The formulas have simply fluttered out of her head. Those ones she leaves.

The sun rises over the science block, falling in molten puddles on the parquet floor. What a day. And maybe the last hot one of the summer. Of the year. Not a day to sit in a stifling exam room. A day to draw on your face in bean juice.

She reaches the end of the paper and checks it through, correcting a few of the easy mistakes, but leaving at least one six-marker completely blank. Sighing, she turns to gaze out of the window.

Her breath catches.

Miss Zita clears her throat. "OK, ladies, your time is up." She starts saying something about what to do with their papers but it's drowned out by the squeal of Zaina's chair as she thrusts it away from the desk.

Miss Zita frowns in concern. "Are you all right?"

"May I go, Miss?" Zaina replies breathlessly, her eyes flicking to the window to reassure herself that what she's seeing isn't just a product of wishful thinking.

Miss Zita follows her gaze, then she smiles. "Yes, Zaina. You may."

Leaving the exam room, Zaina runs through the bars of light criss-crossing the stairwell and bursts out of the building.

Her feet stick at every step she takes towards the science block, and she wonders if she is in a dream, the sort of terrible treacle-walking dream where you are about to obtain your heart's desire only for it to remain forever out of reach. But it's only that the tarmac has melted in the sun.

Someone has dragged a bin over to the porch and she climbs on to it, wobbling a little as she clambers up on to the asphalt roof. Getting to her feet, she experiences a moment's doubt: was it simply a mirage, heat shimmer magicking up an oasis in the desert?

Then, from the roof, a hand stretches down to her.

The hospital put Nero in an induced coma for three days to make sure there was no brain swelling. When they brought him out of it, Zaina was waiting outside his room, but he was asleep and when she came back he'd already been discharged. His parents took him straight to family in Scotland to recuperate over the summer. They've spoken a couple of times on the phone, but there's not much signal in the depths of the Highlands, and his younger cousins kept interrupting, wanting to play.

He could have taken the resit too, but his mum said, "If almost being murdered while trying to save the life of a fellow student isn't enough for Lancaster, they can go fuck themselves." Zaina's mum laughed like a drain when she heard that and said, "You tell it, girl."

He looks different, paler, more fragile, and hauling her up beside him leaves him breathless. But at least he's smiling, his hair, almost grown back to its usual length, curling around the apples of his cheeks.

"So? How was it?"

She wrinkles her nose. "Well, it didn't go as well as when we almost got incinerated by a psychopath."

"Sorry about that."

"Yeah, it was definitely your fault. Damn you for trying to save people's lives when you should be working out quadratic equations."

A quiet settles around them, as light as air. They have talked so much over the past two years it's as if nothing more needs to be said. As they gaze at one another, time softens and dissolves. Zaina has no idea how long it lasts before voices rise up from the path below. Familiar ones: her friends are coming out of the exam. She wants to speak to them, to find out how it went, to congratulate themselves on passing through this final door into adulthood. Just not yet.

"Oh, wait," Nero says. "I brought bubbly to celebrate."

He dives into the Nike rucksack that has definitely seen better days and draws out two cans of Nisa lemonade.

She laughs. This was the drink of choice among all the Franklyn students, as it's unbelievably cheap.

"Also ice cream, which was probably a bit of mistake actually." He grimaces as he withdraws a cylindrical tub that crumples in his grip.

They lounge on the asphalt, drinking warm 25p lemonade and slurping melted ice cream from the tub, their legs dangling in the blue air. Below them the school is spread out like a model village. Unreachably high above them the sun smiles down from a cloudless sky: a main sequence star with the outward pressure of its thermal expansion, perfectly balancing the inward pressure of gravity. At some point the hydrogen in the core will run out and the star will dim and die. You could work it out but, as long as it's shining, who cares?

There are exactly eleven centimetres between his leg and hers. She knows that because the proximity of their bodies has been dominating her thoughts from the moment she got up here. She called it *trivial shit*, the physical pleasure that two people could take in one another. It isn't trivial. It just isn't the sort of stuff you feel like doing when your life is dominated by catheters and enemas and pain relief, and the smell of death and fear and despair, and your mum crying and your baby sister waking in the night screaming because she doesn't understand what's going on but her baby heart knows that whatever it is it's bad. Touching and being touched by someone warm and beautiful and alive are the last things you're thinking of at those times.

But now, in the syrupy heat of this last breath of summer, when her father's memory has softened and mellowed and with it all the stress and anxiety, it's hard not to think about it. About him.

He's telling her a story about how his cousin got bitten by a moray eel while swimming in Loch Lomond, but although she's smiling she's not really listening, just watching the way his lips form the words, the way his eyes flash with laughter. Eventually he notices and the story peters out, the amusement dying from his eyes.

"What?"

"I just…" she says. "I just wanted to talk. About it. You know?"

His throat ripples as he swallows, then nods.

She takes a deep breath. "People make mistakes, Nero."

"I know, and I'm sorry. You will never know how much."

"Not that. I'm not talking about you and Poppy. Poppy was drunk and you were—"

"A total fucking idiot."

"Hurt. I hurt you."

"It was all my fault. I was totally insensitive and selfish to even bring it up when—"

"Shut up."

He squints into her face, specks of gold glittering between his eyelashes.

She takes another breath. For some reason her lung capacity is less than usual. "You asked me a question then. And I gave you the wrong answer."

She wants to explain more; she wants to tell him that there was something awry with her method. Something that meant the numbers didn't add up, the two sides of the equation didn't balance. And they should, because the values of x and y were exactly the same and always would be. But the answer can be simplified. She puts her hand on his warm chest, leans in to him and corrects the mistake.

High above, the endless blue is disturbed only by the white tick of a seagull's wings as it wheels away towards the horizon.

Acknowledgements

First and foremost, thanks to my agent, Eve White, for getting me back to my YA happy place. Also, to Ludo Cinelli and Steven Evans, for their endless patience, hard work and support.

The Scholastic team are a dream to work with. Thank you to my delightful editor, Tierney Holm. To Harriet Dunlea, who was there to hold my hand during the terrifying school visits. To Sarah Dutton, Ellen Thomson, Wendy Shakespeare, Abby Parker, Jamie Gregory, Isabella Haigh and Jennie Roman for making the copy-edit surprisingly painless. Also, huge gratitude to Yasmin Morrissey for signing me and making my year.

Thanks to Molly Milton, editorial consultant and first reader, for ensuring I didn't make any cringey linguistic errors.

To clever Becky, who had the desk beside mine during my multiple-choice GCSE chemistry exam and wrote nice and clearly.

And finally, sympathy and solidarity to all the suffering GCSE and A-level students out there. This too shall pass.

YOU BETTER WATCH OUT

SARAH NAUGHTON

By the time he is himself again dusk has fallen and it is snowing. The temperature has plummeted and his legs are almost too numb to get up. Reeling about the little clearing, he punches himself in the arms and torso, forcing the blood that has rushed to enfold his shattered heart to flow back into his muscles. He has a job to do.

His nails tear away as he thrusts through the first layers of frost-hardened soil, but the deeper earth yields more easily, retaining even now some of the warmth of autumn. He pauses to stare at the blood welling in the nail beds, like crimson varnish. For a moment he can almost smell it, the intoxicating, secret scent of it. Her fingers draped over his wrist as he strokes the brush along her nails. And then the burning chemical smell of the stripper: the fleeting moment of forbidden glamour over.

In the distance, church bells are calling people for midnight Mass.

This will be his Christmas gift to her.

He glances over to where she lies, unable to extinguish the childish hope that she might yet stir. But the first flakes of snow have settled on a cheek no longer warm enough to melt them, and frost has crept over her amber eyes. Their opaque gaze is focused on something far away, too far for him to reach.

He talks to her as he digs, bestowing upon her the grave goods of their memories. But they run out too soon – there should have been so many more – and then he toils in silence.

Sometime later he climbs out of the sunken bed he has made for her. The full moon has covered it with a silver sheet.

As he lifts her into his arms she seems to sigh into his chest and for a moment he stands there, breathing, as the snow drifts like confetti down through the bare branches of the trees.

On shaking legs he carries her across to the slot in the dark Welsh earth, grunting as he lays her down. She is a weight now. He smiles to think of how he will tease her. Afterwards, when they are together again. When he has done what he needs to do.

It's so cold and she's wearing nothing but a T-shirt and jeans. The T-shirt is baggy, to swamp the body she made for herself: the jeans are tight, leaving cruel marks on her soft flesh. There are other marks too, ugly black stains on the parts of her that lay on the hard ground. The blood is no longer flowing into the atriums of her heart or out of the ventricles. They learned that together, breath mingling, heads touching over the textbook. He smiles at the memory and his frozen skin crackles like wax.

He wants to wrap her up in his jacket, keep her warm in that frigid earth, but then when they find her they will know. And he doesn't want them to know. Not straight away. Because there are things he must do first.

For a long time he sits on the edge of her bed. She is asleep. That's all. A slumbering seed, waiting for spring.

Finally he takes up a fistful of soil. His bloody hand is numb so he doesn't feel the grains slipping between his fingers to dust her cheek. He takes another, and another, watching her features soften and disappear. A handful of earth disturbs the neck of her T-shirt and something catches in the moonlight. Her necklace. He reaches forward. On it is her ring and the key. He unfastens the chain, slips both off into his palm, then refastens it.

When he is done there is a slight rise in the land that might betray her resting place to anyone venturing off the dog walkers' path. He cannot bring himself to stamp it down so he lies on his stomach and lets the earth subside beneath him. With his ear pressed to the soil, he thinks he can hear her whispering. He answers her, making promises.

He's surprised to see the shadow of his profile on the dead leaves. It's morning. Getting to his feet, he vomits until his stomach is empty, even of bile, until he can't breathe, until the blood vessels burst in his eyes and the rising sun becomes a disc of blood, until he thinks, thank you, God, *that he will die too.*

But he doesn't die.

As he staggers back through the woods to where his mother's car is parked, he can hear the church bells ringing out for Christmas Day.

Wednesday December 1

The school lockers are about as far from the 11S form room as it's possible to get, so Eleri only ever goes there first and last thing. Most people do the same, and at 8.25 the corridor is rammed and noisy as hell, but somehow she manages to squeeze her way through and feed the combination into her padlock.

The gaggle of popular girls are squealing as slips of red and white striped paper tumble from their open locker doors. These are the invitations for the upper school Christmas Party, or "dance cards", as the head of year insists on calling them. They read:

Dear...
    Will you be my juggling partner at the Cirque De Elsinore House on December 15?
    From...

Then beneath a dotted line a new section reads:

Dear...
    I would love to clown around with you!
    Or
    It's not trap-easy to say this, but no thanks!
From...

You're supposed to collect one from reception, fill it in and slip it inside the locker of the person you want to invite, then they're supposed to tear off the strip at the bottom, cross out the response that doesn't apply and post it back in your locker. By the look of things the popular girls will be having to send quite a few *trap-easy* replies.

"I'd love to see your big top, Tamara!" guffaws a jock as he tramps past on the way to the hall.

"And I'd love to see your head bitten off by a tiger," the girl retorts and the slim blonde herd sashays off.

Two lockers down, Eleri's best friend is gathering her books.

"Hey, Cal," Eleri calls. "How many invites did you get this year?"

Cal gives a lobotomized grin, "Oh, about a million! How about you, El?"

"Same as last year." She swings the locker open to reveal its cavernous interior, empty but for books and a postcard from her aunt Lynne.

"Don't worry," Cal says with faux brightness. "When

they get their rejections from that lot" – she nods after the popular girls, their long brown legs disappearing through the hall doors – "they'll move to the next level down. And then the next and the next, and the class pets, and then us!"

The crowd is starting to disperse as everyone makes their way to the hall, but Eleri and Calista have promised to wait for Beni, who's always late out of morning drama club, because he has a crush on the teacher. Feeling eyes on her Eleri turns, expecting to see him walking up the corridor. But instead finds herself staring into the glinting blue eyes of Ras Mandip.

She's so amazed that for a moment she just stares back at him.

Though their lockers are only two columns apart, Eleri might have been invisible for all the attention Ras has paid her over the past year. But now he's actually looking at her. And not just looking. The corners of his lips are bent in a faint smile.

Eleri jumps as hands descend on her shoulders. "Ready to pick our Secret Santas then, people? I swear if I don't get someone half decent-looking this year there will be a *rampage*."

The Father Christmas hat balanced on Beni's Afro looks like it came from the pound shop, but he carries it off with his usual panache. "And if I get *anything* pink or sparkly, I'm going straight to pastoral care."

They join the herd moving in the direction of the sports hall.

"It shouldn't be compulsory," Calista grumbles. "I've got way too many things to be worrying about than what crappy gift to buy some total stranger."

"Christmas socks," Beni suggests, linking her arm. "You can't go wrong, especially if they light up and play 'Jingle Bells'."

"Whoever I pick this year, they're getting Quality Street," Eleri says.

They emerge into the chill of the playground and she folds her arms against the cold. Ras is in the queue to get through the doors of the gym, leaning his elbow on the head of his annoying friend Teddy P.

After a whole year of barely speaking to me, why would he suddenly catch my eye? Eleri wonders. It probably wasn't deliberate.

The gym smells of feet and BO and old rubber. The morning sunlight pouring through the high, narrow windows makes the parquet glimmer and throws out long shadows behind the students gathered in their various cabals. The jocks scuff the line marks, chatting in gruff voices and occasionally uttering *her her her* laughs. The bad kids (Ras Mandip front and centre) lean against the crash mats looking bored. The popular girls sit on the floor with their knees pulled up, playing with their hair. The hockey team is gathered on the other side of the room and Eleri smiles as the centre back glances in her direction, but her team member's eyes just skim over her.

You would never know someone was missing. There

isn't even a gap where she should have been because the school has filled her space with a new kid.

"It's freezing in here," Calista complains. "I hope this doesn't take too long."

"Who do you want, then?" Beni raises an eyebrow.

"I couldn't care less," Cal grumbles.

"I want Daniel or James C, or that new boy. If I get Daniel I'll get him a new cricket box."

Calista wrinkles her nose. "Yuck."

"Not at all. I care about the integrity of his testicles." Beni sticks out his lower lip and blows the Santa hat pom-pom away from his forehead. It gives an elven tinkle. "What about you, El? Who do you want?" He winks at her over Calista's head.

Eleri shrugs, but her eyes automatically flit to the crash mats.

"Right!" Miss Merrion yells over the hubbub. "Are we all ready for some festive fun?"

There are equal numbers of groans and cheers.

"Who wants to go first?" Miss Merrion gives a wry smile as she shakes the plastic bin on the trestle table in front of her, knowing she will have to start summoning people by name.

But then a hand shoots up from the kids lolling against the crash mats: "Me, miss!" Those around him laugh, but now the gangly frame straightens and Ras Mandip lopes towards the table. His trousers are too short and his shirt is flapping and the skin fade he got on one side of his head, the one he was suspended for, is just starting to grow out. You can see his ridiculously gorgeous eyelashes from the back of the room.

On the way past the gaggle of nerds he snatches a pair of glasses from one of the girls and puts them on top of his head.

"He is such a dick," Calista mutters.

As he nears the trestle table, Miss Merrion's frown melts: Eleri guesses it's because he is treating her to one of his beaming smiles. None of the teachers can stay angry at Ras for long, which is a source of constant irritation to the more strident parents who are always marching in to complain about him disrupting classes.

"Be sensible, please, Ras," Miss Merrion murmurs.

Eleri holds her breath, waiting for him to do something, but instead he just leans over the wrapping-paper-covered bin, biting his lip in exaggerated concentration as he rifles through the slivers of paper inside. Then he gives a subtle flick of his head and the glasses slide off and fall in.

"Oh bother!" he cries, and before Miss Merrion can stop him he has taken the bin from her hands and is delving inside.

"Ras..." the teacher warns, at the clear attempt to sabotage proceedings.

"I have to find them, miss. They're Jeany's. Aha!"

He extracts the glasses with a flourish, and with them a slip of paper.

On the way back to the crash mats, the paper hidden

in his closed fist, Ras tucks the glasses gently over Jeany's coarse red curls, and her cheeks turn the same colour as her hair. As he rejoins his friends, Teddy P joshes him, trying to snatch the strip of paper from his hand, but Ras screws it into a ball with his long fingers, then puts it into his mouth, grimaces, and swallows it down.

"Not fair!" one of the rugby boys shouts. "He was looking at the names!"

But Miss Merrion shouts over him, "Next!"

Other students trickle up to the table. Some respond to their chosen name with poker faces, others are obviously pleased or horrified. The nerds slink up and scurry away, then the jocks approach en masse.

"*Oh man,*" sings a voice from the crash mats. "*Look at those cavemen go…*"

Eleri's mouth twitches.

The rest of the crash-mat kids go up then amble out of the hall, laughing and grimacing over their slips of paper. Ras doesn't look at her as he passes.

"Come on," Calista says. "Let's get this over with."

They join the queue, shuffling through the shafts of dusty sunlight. Calista picks. Then Beni. And then it's Eleri's turn.

She walks forward, towards the gaping mouth of the bin.

"Go on, Eleri," Miss Merrion says, and suddenly Eleri is back there, last year, standing at the same table in front of the same plastic bin, picking out a slip of paper inscribed with the name *Nina M*.

"I don't know who this is," she had whispered, frowning down at the tiny, neat hand.

"The new girl," Miss Merrion murmured. "Over by the monkey bars. Black hair, glasses."

Walking back to her friends, Eleri glanced over. Nina M stood alone, shoulders hunched, head bent as if desperately trying to shrink her oversized frame, to make herself invisible to the sharp eyes of the popular girls and hot boys. Eleri felt an immediate rush of pity. She wouldn't have it easy here, looking like that. They'd make up names for her: *the Hulk* or *the Blob*, or something similarly cruel and unimaginative.

She resolved then to get Nina M something really nice for her Secret Santa present. Perhaps the new girl was into something, like art or books. Eleri would give it some proper thought, she decided, get to know Nina a little better, and do everything she could to make her first Christmas at Elsinore House a happy one.

But Nina never made it to Christmas. On December 15th of last year the new girl went missing, and despite the coverage on the local news, the posters slapped on every bus stop and lamp post, the flyers handed out by an army of volunteers, she might as well have vanished off the face of the earth.

"Eleri?"

"Sorry. I was miles away."

Miss Merrion shakes the bin. The slips of paper whisper against her fingertips: *pick me, pick me.* Eleri grasps one and snatches her hand out.

As she walks quickly away to join her friends, she glances at the note and feels a rush of relief. It's Beni.

Wednesday is pasta day and Eleri gets a ladleful of flabby spaghetti in a glutinous brown sauce that smells like a laundry basket full of socks. She, Cal and Beni head for their usual spot, a small round table in the far corner of the room, away from the hustle and noise of the long tables. They've been sitting here since the three of them joined the school from the same primary five years ago.

As they pass she doesn't glance at Ras's table, but she can hear his friend Kika nagging him to tell her who he picked.

Beni falls into step beside her. "I reckon he deliberately dropped the glasses so he could choose. Perhaps it was you, El." He waggles his eyebrows.

"Yeah, right. He hasn't spoken to me in a year."

"Maybe he realized the error of his ways."

"He was probably going for Tamara George."

"You're probably right." Beni sighs. "I would totally kill for her lips. And eyes. And hair."

"And money."

They've reached the table. It would seat four but Calista always moves the fourth chair away to give them more room.

"So-o-o…" Beni drawls as they sit down. "Who did we all get?"

"Can't say," Eleri says, poking the greasy tentacles of her meal.

"Er, why?" Calista looks at her suspiciously.

"It's in the name! *Secret* Santa."

Cal rolls her eyes.

"So who did *you* get?" Beni says.

Calista's lip curls. "Matthew H."

"Ooh, he's hot!"

"If you like dumb jocks."

"We *all* like dumb jocks! I got that girl with the eyebrows that join up."

"Who cares? It's all cringe," Cal says, forking up a tangle of spaghetti.

Beni starts talking about football. About how the new boy has signed up for the team and he hopes he's better than their current striker who couldn't hit a barn door at five paces. Beni can talk for England and doesn't require much in the way of a response. Soon his voice merges into the general hubbub around them.

"... and supposedly he's a Millwall fan. What kind of normal human being supports *Millwall*? I mean, you'd have to be..."

Something makes Eleri look up.

Ras's eyes are all wrong. How many other Indian boys with jet-black hair and dark skin have aquamarine eyes? They're so clear as well, like the irises are tinted glass or seawater, and you might see silver fish swimming behind them. She knows all this because, for the few seconds it takes for the thoughts to pop into her mind, those improbable eyes are looking right into hers.

*

Sarah grew up in Somerset with her mum and a selection of short-lived hamsters. Here she developed her lifelong love of reading, as there wasn't much else to do.

She studied English literature at university, which perfectly prepared her for her numerous roles in hospitality and catering. She has also been an advertising copywriter, a cheesemonger, a carpet cleaner and a writer (her favourite so far).

She lives in London with her husband and two sons, who enjoy reading as much as she enjoys steam-cleaning chewing gum off a Turkish rug.